A Thousand Drops of Rain

A Thousand Drops of Rain

A Sojourn into Southeast Asian Surrealism

Peter Crittenden

A Thousand Drops of Rain: A Sojourn in Southeast Asian Surrealism

by Peter Crittenden

ISBN 978-1956904-10-9

Printed in the United States of America

Published by Blacksmith LLC
Fayetteville, North Carolina

www.BlacksmithPublishing.com

Direct inquiries and/or orders to the above web address.

Contents

Chapter

1 – The Python.. 1

2 – The Duck Feather King 17

3 – Brick on a Birthday Cake 47

4 – A Social Media Success Story 63

5 – The Survivor 80

6 – Pictures in a Gallery 93

7 – Exorcism 103

8 – Dieter & the Giant Collider 114

9 – Dirt Bag 135

10 – The Machine 167

11 – Down South 182

12 – The Cement Business 197

13 – Casino 226

About the Author 240

Chapter 1

The Python

"Inside every person you know, there's a person you don't know . . ." - Anonymous

It was going to be a hot day but for now Mike enjoyed the cool of the morning, sitting at his special table in the corner of the open-air restaurant that opened out onto the veranda. Every morning Mike would dedicate several hours to writing, or at least try to. Adding to Mike's writer's block was no shortage of distractions. From where he worked at a quiet corner of the large veranda looking out over the jungled cliffs, there was always something going on. He'd look up and see the colony of monkeys making war against the pack of dogs that hung around the compound. Tropical birds screeching added a constant texture of sound. Way out in the distance a large sailboat crossed the shining waters of the Andaman Sea.

This is where the Andaman Sea begins its run southward to the Straits of Malacca. The blue waters are dotted with hundreds of golden-sand rimmed islands of emerald green. The islands have fantastic shapes, one shaped like a the handle of a shovel or some other implement, sticking up from the water, another like a woman's breasts.

As he struggled with plot ideas, Mike didn't see it at first. Instead he noticed his dog Loodi, down by his feet. Loodi - a young, short-haired dachshund – was shaking like a leaf. The dog's eyes transfixed on something out in front of Mike's table. Mike followed the dog's gaze to the banyan tree just beyond the veranda, near the spirit house, and what he saw confused him at first. There was a shimmering on the bark of the many-trunked tree, like water flowing down; water, on top of water. It didn't make any sense, and it dazzled the eye. Mike looked again, and then again. Water flowing down . . . water . . . water on top of water . . .

Then Mike shook his head and saw it for what it was; a huge python was slithering down the banyan tree, not ten feet away of him. The python's head was as big as a football. Incredible muscles rippling beneath its black, brown and tan scales, like something other-worldly. It was the sunlight glinting off its scales that created the hypnotic effect of water flowing down, water on top of water . . . water . . . on top of water . . . water . . . flowing down . . .

As huge as the creature was, Mike felt no sense of fear. Pythons are actually quite gentle, and as huge as this one was, Mike was sure it posed no immediate danger to him. Instead he watched, fascinated, the gigantic serpent's coils twisting, rippling beneath its scales, like the exaggerated arm muscles of a Michelangelo sculpture.

Then Mike noticed giant serpent's eyes, focusing right on the little dog Loodi. The snake's forked tongue going in and out appeared almost to be salivating in anticipation of its intended meal.

Mike scooped up Loodi and quickly moved inside. As he went in, one of the maids went past him with a broom to perform her daily chore on the veranda. There was a scream as the maid encountered the monster, and she quickly reappeared inside the dining room, white as a ghost and chattering excitedly. She was speaking so fast Mike couldn't understand what she was saying, apart from the Thai word for snake: '*ngoo*'.

The police were called, and they appeared on the scene quite quickly. Probably out of curiosity, Mike assumed. The snake itself remained in the banyan tree, seemingly oblivious of the tumult it had created in the compound.

But the cops didn't want anything to do with the reptile; they were as unwilling to approach it as any of the domestic staff. The local snake farm was called: "Are you missing a thirty-foot python? No? Well, do you want one?" While they waited for the team from the snake farm to arrive to take charge of the beast, the snake remained quite docile in amongst the many trunks of the banyan tree.

Mike was interested in how the herpetologists intended to capture the monster. He'd handled smaller pythons and was aware of their powerful strength. If one of these snakes wrapped itself around something – a tree, or a living creature - it was impossible to pull it off.

The men from the snake farm arrived, and they brought a bamboo cage with them – about six foot long, by four foot wide – stoutly fabricated, containing a young pig, squealing its unhappiness. They simply placed the cage near the base of the banyan tree, and everybody repaired to the veranda while the snake became acquainted with the piglet.

The enormous serpent became aware of the pig. It lifted its head and slowly moved in the direction of the cage. It easily entered between the upright bamboo bars of cage, and proceeded to wrap itself around the poor pig, which squealed a few more times until the breath was literally squeezed out of it by the mighty constrictor. The pig's last moments were punctuated by the snapping of bones. The slaying of its prey accomplished, the python stretched its jaws wide, dislocating them, and swallowed the piglet whole.

The python then attempted to make its way back toward the jungle. However, a huge lump in its midsection – the yet-to-be digested piglet – prevented the python from moving between the bamboo bars of the cage.

Resigning itself to the situation, the giant reptile became sluggish as it began to digest its huge meal. The team from the snake farm was able to lift it, cage and all, and place it in the back of their truck.

Another story no one would ever believe, except that Mike had pictures and the story would make it onto his blog. Unfortunately, another day's attempt at writing was shot.

Mike returned to his special table in the corner of the hotel's open-air restaurant. A couple of tourists huddled together on the other side of the restaurant, planning their day over coffee, toast and eggs. One of the secrets of the success of Mike's offbeat hotel was offering a western-style breakfast – and making this feature well known through advertising and in the travel blogs. Thai cuisine is great, but for the adventure travelers Mike's menu offered a break from the otherwise endless routine of fish sauce and chili peppers that punctuates every meal in Thailand, including breakfast.

The other secret to Mike's success was the fantastic view; a panorama of the sparkling waters of the Andaman Sea, interspersed with emerald green islands. The hotel was built against the side of a hill, a series of traditional Thai houses up on stilts, with decking connecting the buildings. The houses were not all in a line, they followed the contours of the hillside, and so guests effectively had detached bungalows with areas to relax and sunbathe. Mike had cleverly created several small swimming pools between the hillside and the cluster of buildings, offering guests multiple areas to relax in complete privacy.

The main building itself was a large *"baan"* – a traditional Thai house built up on large timber piles. The main offices and the bar were on the upper floor, which was like a ship's deck. Beneath this deck was the hotel's reception area, the kitchen and the restaurant. The floor was a vast polished concrete slab, leading out to the wide veranda overlooking the cliff and the beach down below.

The bar Mike had created was a traditional pub - no easy feat this far off the beaten path - very popular with the local population of ex-pats. Mike officially named it The Long Bar; it was L-shaped but straightened out it came to about a half a football field in length. A very long bar, hence 'The Long Bar'.

Mike's inspiration was an oasis of sanity, an island of calm in the otherwise chaotic bright neon lights and loud rock music of usual Thai night life. And here came the irony of it all.

With half his life behind him, ergo half his life ahead of him, Mike had decided to make his home in the tropics of Southeast Asia, to escape the chaos of life in the west. It was his lifelong dream to write, and his new life as the owner of this unorthodox hotel would hopefully give him the time now to write.

Or so he thought.

A writer needs more than time and place, he needs inspiration. There was time enough in the mornings, it was the second thing that plagued Mike. What to write about? Characters were easy – he'd met enough of them in his life. Themes? Somewhere between science fiction and fantasy, a touch of the noir genre, with Joseph Conrad and Somerset Maugham overtones. Settings? In the tropics, of course. What eluded Mike was a plot of any kind . . .

There was a constant stream of ideas going across his consciousness, little thirty-second clips that seemed to capture an entire book-length concept, but one after another he rejected them all. Too much science fiction out there, bookstores seemed saturated with the stuff. As far as pure action-adventure went, sure a yarn had to have some action in it but Mike didn't want to be labeled and then stuck into a genre.

Back to the basics, he thought of Conrad, which fit perfectly with his surroundings. The theme was there, but somehow a plot that fit with the tropical environment failed to present itself. The hoots and howls of the monkeys in the lush forested hillside, the calls and screeches of the birds, the sunlight glinting off the distant Andaman Sea, the clink of silverware on china, and the ultimate distraction of a silent Oriental girl placing a cup and saucer by his work station and retreating so as not to disturb his thought train.

Throughout this frustrating experience, a singular theme ran through his mind, revolving around a personality so vivid and strong he could not shake it. A blonde, in her late thirties or early forties, showed up at the hotel. She wore a blue sarong and a simple white cotton top; she almost looked like a nun. She moved in, became a long-term resident of one of the bungalows, even came to The Long Bar in the evenings. She gradually became part of the local scene.

In this almost dream-like storyline growing in Mikes mind, he didn't even know her name, although she certainly had a name. She became known as simply 'The Blonde Woman', and she was part of the local ex-pat scene. She was not there on vacation; she was an overseas contractor. She left for several months at a time, only to return between contracts. In this way she had something in common with several of the guys, and this led to her acceptance at the bar as 'one of the guys'.

The crazy thing was that so many of guys wound up in Asia to get away from white women, seeking to live out their fantasy of subservient, doll-like Oriental women, sexually exotic; the 'China Doll' stereotype. Never mind that this stereotype didn't match up to reality. Mike suspected a part of the allure was the language barrier, thus negating the requirement for conversation, or at least reducing it. So why was this blonde creature haunting him? Try as he might he could not shake her from his thoughts.

As he sought a storyline, the blonde woman continued to pester his imagination. He could almost see her sitting at one of the tables as he struggled to write, squeezing a slice of lemon over a plate of papaya, or enjoying a cup of rich, dark Thai coffee; thick and sweet as treacle, which somehow worked in the tropical mornings. The more he struggled to get her out of his mind, the more prominent she became. She became a presence, like a ghost. He even imagined her taking walks along the path that led down the cliff to the beach.

Perhaps it was inevitable that this spirit-like being appear in his dreams. In a strange, semi-lucid fantasy, the Blonde Woman joined him beneath the mosquito netting. Aware this was a dream, almost awake, Mike turned from side to side in a fever-like delirium. They became lovers in a most fantastic way.

Beyond the fact that it occurred in a dream, there was an other-worldly sensation to this encounter. Time slowed, the very atmosphere felt hot, heavy and dense. As they grappled it was almost as if the blood in Mike's veins was replaced with molten lead. The Blonde's muscles rippled beneath her skin, and her body coiled about him like a constricting snake, squeezing the life force from him in exchange for pleasure delivered.

She gave him everything and anything any man could want of a woman, so much so that when he awoke he was bathed in sweat. Mike stared into the ink-like tropical darkness; there was no sense of time or dimension. Exhausted, he tossed and turned, tortured by the nocturnal visit. Sleep finally came, a merciful deep, dark sleep like the sleep of the dead.

And in the morning as he struggled to write, she again entered his imagination. Mike sat at his table at the edge of the open restaurant where the veranda met the jungle. As usual he imagined the Blonde Woman sitting at a table at the other side of the café. This time the image of the Blonde Woman became a hallucination; she got up from her table, walked over and sat down before him. "That was not supposed to happen last night," she said simply.

"No, of course not," Mike replied. The serving girl witnessing this one-sided conversation knew now what she had long suspected; Khun Mike was *"ba"* - going mad in the tropics, like white men are prone to do.

The story continued. Mike's gang at the bar came to him; they had done some homework on the Internet, looked up the Blonde Woman's name. It did not matter that she did not have a name – she was a pure creature of fiction dwelling solely inside Mike's mind. She was notorious in contractor circles, apparently, her name was mentioned in the reports of an investigation. There were rumors of large-scale black marketing, and she was associated with the deaths of two American contractors under extremely mysterious circumstances. Mike's friends warned him: "She's some kind of female assassin."

Mike shrugged it off. It was too crazy. In the fantastic internal conversation that now consumed his consciousness, he stated, "It's only fiction, she's only a figment of my imagination."

And yet she was there. She moved about wherever he went. During every waking moment in the course of his day, he could see her out of the corner of his eye.

Creative writing with this kind of mental burden was out of the question. Mike needed to leave this fantasy world and immerse himself in the here and now. A construction project seemed a good idea; Mike decided to create a new level to the patio, another pool one level down, between the hotel complex and the beach. This meant a terrace to be dug into the slope of the cliff, foundations piles to be driven, cement to be poured, and all of this to be done before the monsoon rains arrived.

Nothing like a spot of good hard work to sweat out crazy, destructive thoughts.

For Mike, part of the fun and enjoyment of living in southern Thailand was the simplicity of everything. Construction permits were practically unheard of, and there was no lack of resources. Cement was plentiful, albeit not cheap but not expensive either. If he needed manpower all he need do was speak up and the laborers would arrive, construct little dwellings of bamboo and live on site until the work was done.

Because of the lay of the hillside it was impossible to get any kind of vehicle in there; every aspect of the project had to be done by physical labor. Mike immersed himself in the project, hoisting fifty-pound bags of cement on his shoulder, or toting heavy baskets of gravel alongside the Thai workers as they made their way down the steep and narrow path to the cutout in the hill where the new pool would be. Flexing his muscles in the sun and wiping his face with a sweat rag was just the kind of therapy Mike needed to erase the strange woman from his thoughts.

The project proceeded. Major construction was completed on schedule and ahead of the rainy season. The pool featured a wide flat area at the outer edge where the pool water overflowed down into a gutter, to be recirculated back. For swimmers or people lounging poolside, the illusion was an "endless horizon" that appeared to be one with the sea in the distance, a beautiful scene framed by coconut palms. All that remained was some fancy tile work and a statue to spout water out; a touch of the exotic east. Mike was proud of his handiwork, and the crazy female being haunting his imagination seemed to have gone away.

The physical work of building the pool out of the way, Mike took up the habit of a morning run along the beach followed by a dip in the new pool. Afterwards he would lie out poolside and the sun would dry him. He found this an effective exercise to cleanse the mind and face the challenge of writing. And so it was this morning, as he made his way back up to the café.

The ritual of the coffee and the laptop ensued until the distractions overcame his ability to focus. It was a

Wednesday and there was a bit of administrative work to do; might as well get up and get it done. Leena-wan, the Chinese girl who worked as cashier, was least patient of all with Mike's creative struggles. Business first, and who had any time to read books that didn't involve columns of figures, much less to pretend to try to write them?

The books attended to, Mike considered what to do with the rest of his day. A random idea came to him straight out of the blue; how about a trip to the snake farm to look at "his" giant python? It was only thirty minutes up the road. Mike grabbed his wallet and his phone and went out to the jeep.

The snake farm was a field office of the larger institute in Bangkok. Most of the snakes they kept were venomous, for the extraction of snake venom to produce anti-venom. But they also kept a collection of exotic snakes as a tourist attraction. Mike's python wasn't the only large constrictor there.

"Oh, *Khun* Mike," the director said, "Something very unusual happen. Your python not here."

"What, did you send it to Bangkok?"

"No, it get out. Escape."

Mike didn't understand. How could the python escape its enclosure? The big constrictors all lived in a large pit, almost thirty meters across, with high walls and a moat.

There was no possible way it could get out. And yet the snake farm workers all insisted that it had gotten away.

Oh well, another day burned out. Shame, because it really was a magnificent snake.

When Mike returned to the hotel there was some business that required his attention at the reception counter. Mike looked up across the counter to see a new guest approaching the reception area. She was a blonde, forty-something. Blue sarong, simple white cotton top, and a tan kit bag covered with zippers and plastic buckles just like the overseas contractors carried. "I'd like one of the bungalows," she said.

Mike's jaw dropped.

When Leena Wan finished signing her into the hotel, the Blonde Woman looked up. Mike had composed himself. "You took your time getting here," he said.

"There were a few distractions along the way," she replied, giving him a knowing look. It was as if they already knew each other, and of course in a way they already did. The Blonde Woman hoisted her bag to her shoulder and turned to make her way to the bungalow.

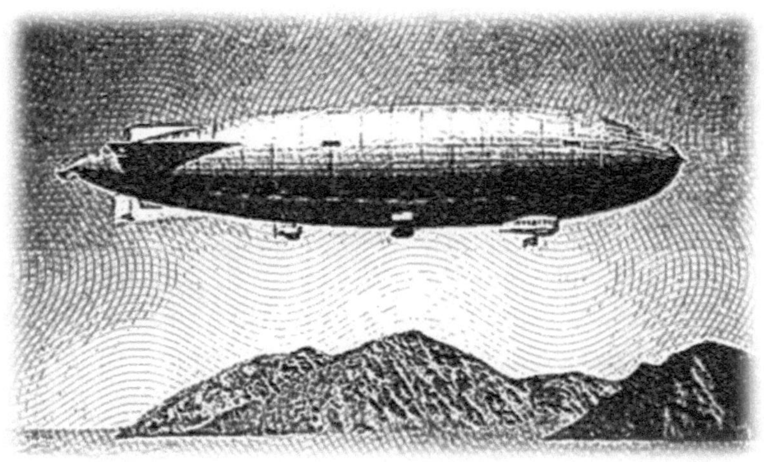

Chapter 2

The Duck Feather King

"This is a story from the old sailing ship days . . ."

The speaker was a distinguished looking gentleman in his sixties, yet still sporting a full head of jet black hair. He reminded Mike of an aging Errol Flynn, or perhaps a David Niven. It was after sundown in The Long Bar, a moonless tropical night beyond the edge of the veranda. The endless booming of the surf hitting the beach at the base of the cliff provided an assurance of . . . eternity.

"In the old days," the gentleman continued, "if a ship sailed across the ocean and made it back with a hull full of spices and other cargo, the profit earned was ten times the value of the ship itself. It was a very lucrative trade.

17

"But sailing wooden ships across the ocean was very hazardous, and of all the ships that set forth, only about half of them made it back."

"That sounds about right," said Mike, "although I've never thought of it before." He topped off the gentleman's whiskey. "This is on the house. Go on."

"Right, so what they would do was this: in the taverns down by the docks, the ships' owners would write the names of their ships on a big chalkboard, and people would place bets on which ships they thought would make it back.

"The ship owners would then take these bets - betting against themselves - until the cost of the ship itself was reached; these bets would be written beneath the name of each ship on the big board.

"That way, if a ship didn't make it back, the replacement cost of the ship was covered. If the ship made it back, the owner would pay out the equivalent of ten percent of his profits, and he'd still have nine times the cost of his initial investment."

"I get it," Mike said. "It was their way of insuring their investments."

"Quite right," the gentleman said. "It was the earliest form of insurance. And because of the way they kept track of these bets on the boards, writing the bets beneath the names of the ships, they called this system – wait for it – 'underwriting'."

The crickets chirped their endless song outside in the inky blackness and the boom, boom, booming of the surf provided a texture of sound to fill the pause.

"This principle of insurance is still in effect today, of course," the gentleman went on. "Insurance, in fact, is the biggest industry on the planet, bigger than oil, even.

"Think of it; there's an insurance aspect to every single part of every ship that crosses the ocean, every single turn of the screw. And of course, an aspect of insurance covers every single part of every single commercial and industrial endeavor under the sun."

Mike wondered where all this was going. That was no reason to be impolite, however.

"You know," Mike stated, "I never thought of it this way. Never thought of it this way at all, but you're absolutely right."

"Well, there are some things that written insurance policies cannot cover. That's where the concept of self-coverage comes in. What happened was, an engineering company was contracted to construct a large power plant – four units, natural gas-fired, two hundred and fifty megawatts – over there in Cambodia." He indicated an easterly direction with a nod of his head, and once again Mike imagined an MGM pirate. "We're talking over 1.5 megawatts, enough to power a good part of the country, which is in the process of developing an industrial base, of course. The scheme would include selling power to Vietnam and Laos, and as a surplus standby for Thailand, which is incredibly energy hungry these days."

"There are all kinds of large machinery that go into a power plant, of course. Well it just so happened that the Thai Electrical Generating Authority had eight of these enormous pumps, left over from a project that had been cancelled, due to a falling out with the World Bank. There was an opportunity, so the lead engineer from the American consulting firm managed to line up a deal.

"The deal was this: his firm would buy the pumps from the Thais, something that consulting firms never do, by the way. But in this case it was the easiest way to pay for the things and get them moving. We're talking a lot of money here, there'd be all kinds of bureaucratic hoops to jump through moving it government to government, down through the ministries, etcetera.

"The American engineer's bosses – the firm's senior executive leadership – saw the deal as a way to get the project moving, and turn a profit along the way, so they gave it the nod. The Thais would recoup their losses, and the Cambodians would be able to get their hands on some very expensive equipment at below cost, and the Americans stood to make a pretty penny. It was a win-win for everyone."

"Right," Mike acknowledged.

"But of course, nothing works that simply in the real world."

"Of course not."

"There was a falling out between the Thais and the Cambodians. You know, the ongoing border war. Now, these wars have been going on since at least the fall of Phnom Penh, back in the seventies. Basically a series of artillery duels, every now and then some light infantry raids across the border, but no big deal. Sure, some people get hurt, but they're more border disputes over real estate, not real wars.

"At this stage of the game, however, those pumps were sitting on the docks at Samut Prakan, and somebody way up high in the Ministry of Industry decided it was a good idea to keep sitting on them."

"Ooh, not good . . ."

"No, not at all. Suddenly the American firm was out a lot of cash, and the future of the project itself was at risk. Everybody was about to lose a lot of money, all over eight pieces of equipment held up on the docks, already bought and paid for."

"That's when I was approached. Was there any way I could get the pumps released for shipment?"

"Okay," Mike said. He was actually following the story, in between tending to drinks up and down the bar.

"But I'm retired! I told them. You speak fluent Thai, they said, you're an engineer, you understand the machinery, and you know your way around down there, besides.

"I read the business pages, of course, and I saw there was over forty million tied up in that project. I estimated the cost of those pumps somewhere around one to two percent of that – these are really big things, about thirty feet tall and as wide as this room – so I knew how much was at stake, and how to price my services accordingly. So of course I said I'd do it."

"Of course."

"I was instructed to go to the American Embassy and meet with a certain gentleman there. I had to give up my British passport at the entrance and get escorted into the security side of the embassy. They showed me into an office, introduced me to this younger fellow, obvious ex-military type. He looked at me and said, 'I don't know who you are Mister, but you must be somebody important, because I was instructed to sign over this suitcase full of cash to you.'

"We always see in the movies, how one million dollars' cash easily fits into a suitcase. There's nothing fantastic about it. You can get such a sum into a relatively small package if you stack ten thousand $100 bills.

"Uh, how much was it?" Mike asked.

"I counted it – the gentleman insisted on it. I don't want to say how much I signed for – there are currency laws, after all – but let me just say that the pile came to five percent of the project, when we were done counting it. Turns out my mental math regarding the project was spot on. What we were looking at was basically how much it took the consulting firm to cover of a very lucrative contract, of course; remember the underwriting of the ships? They'd stuck their necks out when they'd gotten involved in purchasing the pumps off the shelf, as it were. The consultants would usually never be involved in such an aspect, but when the original deal went down apparently someone had gotten greedy. Now they had to cough up the cash.

"The young man – he must have been some kind of intelligence officer or security type - said again, 'I don't know who you are, Mister, and I don't want to know. I'm just doing my job.' I'm sure he had all kinds of exotic ideas about who I was, because I don't even have an American accent!

"I thanked him and took the suitcase, walked down Wireless Road to my hotel, dragging my bag behind me on its little rollers. In a little shop in the lobby I picked up two smaller bags that would fit inside the larger bag, then I went up to my room and did a little re-distribution."

At this point Mike was fully absorbed in the gentleman's story.

"The next stop was the docks at Samut Prakan, of course."

"Oh yeah, the pumps." Mike was still drooling over the thought of all that cash.

"The ship they were supposed to be loaded upon was in port, but the pumps were sitting right there on the dockside. The big derricks that move the cargo were sitting idle. I was stopped as I walked across the docks towards the ship. 'Sir,' they told me, 'you cannot go onto this ship while it is being refueled."

"My good man," I replied, "do you mean to tell me that as captain I cannot board my own ship?"

"Ha!" Mike laughed, practically snorting beer through his nose.

"The ruse worked. They stood aside and I went up the gangplank, suitcase in my hand. On the bridge, the real captain asked me, 'Who are you?'

"I'm the one who's going to get your cargo loaded and your vessel underway," I told him, "and if you and I could meet in your office, I'd like to share with you one hundred thousand reasons why you should let me get a cabin on board for the trip over to Battambang."

"Five percent of the five percent," Mike stated.

"Quite right," the gentleman replied. To Mike, he was looking more and more like a swashbuckler as his tale unfolded.

"I assured the captain I was not a fugitive of any kind, showed him my British passport with current visas in it, and invited him to speak with the British embassy regarding my status in the Kingdom. No worries there – the charge d'affairs is a friend of mine.

"For his cooperation, I presented the captain with one of the little suitcases. That little bit of business out of the way, I stashed the large suitcase – and what was in it – in a locker in the cabin provided, and then with the other little suitcase in hand, I went back on shore to see the harbor master about loading up those pumps."

"Back on the docks I was informed that the Harbor Master was at his station – they pointed to a control tower -like structure on an island in the middle of the estuary, but that he was asleep, it being early afternoon. The siesta hour, you know. I told them that the Harbor Master was a close personal friend of mine and that he would be very pleased to see me.

"This was not quite untrue. He wasn't yet a friend of mine, but after he took a look at what I had for him in the little suitcase, he certainly would be.

"I was able to take a launch out to the little island and visit the Harbor Master. I told him there was a special urgency, that we needed his permission to load the cargo onto my ship while it was being fueled. Notice I managed to avoid the subject of what the cargo itself was, you see. I laid the little suitcase on his desk and told him that I understood he could not accept gifts in his official capacity, but that if I mistakenly left behind my bag, he might become aware of a hundred thousand reasons to give me permission to load my cargo and sail on the tide.

"As you can imagine, the Harbor Master saw it my way, and was very cooperative. The pumps were loaded aboard the ship, and we sailed that afternoon."

"Problem solved!" Mike exclaimed.

"Not quite. Now there was another problem."

"Oh?"

"Well, like I said, there are currency laws, regarding the movement of large sums of cash across international borders."

"Oh, right."

"This is where my knowledge of machinery came in handy. Pumps involve shafts, bearings and all kinds of seals and gaskets. The pumps' impellers must be rotated, at least ninety degrees a day, or the bearings would freeze, lock up. This gave me reason to be in the cargo bays. I went about each pump and made a chalk mark, indicating the position of rotation. While I was at it, I had access the inspection hatches on the pumps, which just so happened to be a perfect compartment for a large suitcase. If someone had reason to place a suitcase within such a compartment, that is. And of course, one of the pumps was marked differently than the others. To the unknowing observer, the chalk marks meant nothing, of course."

"Of course," Mike agreed.

"The trip to Battambang was uneventful; the Gulf of Siam is a relatively calm body of water. Quite a pleasant cruise, actually. We anchored offshore in the waters sheltered by the many large islands and entered the port in the morning.

"The project had its pumps, the consulting firm was off the hook, and for what the pumps were originally priced at in their contract, they'd actually realized half that price in savings for what they'd paid the Thais for the pumps."

"And you had the difference . . ." Mike pointed out.

"Quite. I represented the unwritten clause in their insurance policy, when you think about it. Of course, now there was another problem."

"Oh?"

"Well, like I said, there are those bothersome international currency laws."

"Oh yeah . . ."

"That part of Southeast Asia is still a bit of the old Wild West, you know. There are fortunes to be made, and people willing to do what it takes to make those fortunes."

Mike wasn't sure if he wanted to know any more, but there was something captivating about the gentleman. In any case, he didn't give out the vibe of an outlaw or a desperado. If he was a criminal, he certainly wouldn't be confessing his crimes here at The Long Bar.

"I invested in a duck operation."

"A duck operation?"

"Yes. There's a tremendous international market for duck feathers, apparently. They use them for filling sleeping bags and those big puffed-up jackets you see people walking around in, looking like the Michelin Man."

"Right."

"The operation was already in place, but I was able to provide the cash to help them expand their international operations, get around the Chinese who have this sort of thing wrapped up."

"You were able to launder your cash?"

"Legalize it. Please. Laundering cash is what drug dealers do. There was nothing illegal in what I was doing, I was paid for solving a problem. An honest day's pay for an honest day's work. What I had was to do now was find a creative solution to an unorthodox means of capital gains.

"With the duck feathers I was sitting upon a veritable gold mine. I'd simply bank the profits through my Swiss account, making sure everything was in accordance with all applicable tax laws. The trick is to never get greedy, of course. Never lose sight of the goal, which for me was to simply re-coup the ten percent I had to expend in the course of earning that cash."

"And while I was at it, a lot of people made a lot of money. During the course of events I became the Duck Feather King. My sources – the duck farmers – and everyone all along the way, from the people who boxed up and shipped the duck feathers to the merchant bankers and everyone in between, all were well-paid for their labors."

"Good karma."

"I like to think so."

"So what happened? You still the Duck Feather King?"

"Oh heavens no. As I said, I'm retired. Who needs the stress of running a commercial enterprise like that? And besides, when you're dealing on that level – I was living in a bamboo shack up on stilts right next to the duck farm, mind you – one's constantly got to keep one's wits about them. Who is conspiring to try and shake you down? Will the ducks all fly away? Or heaven forbid get some kind of bird flu? There's a million little things that go across a fellow's mind when he's in the middle of an operation like that. Not least of all the mosquitos, and having to deal with not getting malaria or dengue fever."

"Eventually I reached the point where I was making enough money on the commercial side, selling duck feathers as a bulk commodity to the clothing manufacturers, that I made my pile, replenished what moving those pumps cost me out of the original pile of cash, that is, and legally banked all of it, it was time to make my move."

"Oh? What did you do?"

"I was pleased to hand over the day-to-day duck operation to the farmers who were doing all the work. All I asked – and got in writing – was primary dealer's rights to the duck feathers. But even still, I didn't want to fly directly into Bangkok. There's no end of stories about the Thai authorities bending their business laws to the best of their advantage."

"Right."

"I didn't want to give them the opportunity to waylay me at the airport on even the tiniest hint of some kind of trumped up nonsense while they fish around for their cut. I still had my residency permits and visas in my British passport, of course, so I rode out of Cambodia on the back of a moped. Made it across the border during a lull in the shooting. One of my duck farmers was driving, actually."

"That's it? You cashed out and made it home free? Run for the border?"

"Well, not quite."

"Let me guess – the Thais were pissed about the pumps making their way to Battambang, and sniffing around they figured you were involved?"

"Yes, it's been a bit of a rocky road, I'm afraid. The Ministry of Industry tried connecting me to the pump caper, but there was no paper trail one way or the other. I keep telling them the truth, that I'm in the duck feather business, and nothing they throw at me sticks. It's all been like water off a duck's back, to coin a phrase."

Mike winced at that. "Ouch."

The Duck Feather King raised an eyebrow as he raised his glass in praise of his own witticism. "Here's cheers!"

Mike raised his and they clinked glasses. "Nowadays?" he inquired.

"Well, somebody somewhere decided it was a good idea to have that fellow at the American embassy contact me. You know, the 'I-don't-know-who-you-are-and-I-don't-want-to-know' gentleman."

"Huh?" Mike grunted.

"Yes, quite. It seems now I'd solved their pumps problem, they had another challenge that needed seeing to.

"Of course. What did they want this time?"

"They wanted me to fly a Zeppelin airship down to the South Pole."

"W-h-a-a-a-t?" Mike gasped, incredulous.

"I told him I'm retired, don't you know? I don't do that sort of thing anymore. But of course, he didn't bat an eyelid at that. It seems the Sultan of Brunei had one of these things – they're still around, you know, modern version thereof - and they wanted me to go down, pick it up, and drop it off at the Pole's Amundsen-Scott Research Station. Made it sound as simple as delivering a pizza or something."

"I suppose they figured after the pumps you're their man."

"Yes. Apparently, I'd become their 'Go-To-Guy' for whatever crazy thing they had coming down the pike. I told them, look, all I know about Zeppelins is they were a great act in the Seventies, I've never flown one."

"What did they say to that?"

"Well, the gentleman pointed out that I am one of only three pilots to ever have flown a helicopter at the South

Pole – which is true, by the way – and how much harder can it be?

"Of course, flying a helicopter down there is no easy feat, I told him. For one thing, the South Pole is one of the highest, driest and coldest places on earth. Elevation at the Pole is approximately 9,300 feet above sea level, and there's a mountain range there you'd have to clear, up to 16,000 feet. The cold affects altimeter readings; the average temperature there during the Antarctic 'summer' is minus 25 degrees Celsius, and that quickly drops to minus 50 degrees at altitude. Lord knows what the cold would do to the gas bags on a dirigible."

"I can't even imagine a Zeppelin going down to the South Pole," Mike said, incredulous.

"Yes, and the winds blow like you can't imagine. Antarctic winds flow down the coastal slopes under the influence of gravity. Speeds of these katabatic winds have been recorded up to two hundred miles per hour."

"Good God! What were they thinking? An airship can't negotiate those kind of winds!"

"That's exactly what I told them. But they were adamant about their project – the airship, they told me, was special. An advanced design. Carbon fiber frame, synthetic fabrics, complete modern computerized avionics package – a completely different thing from the old Zeppelins or even the modern airships in use today. For one thing, it had jet engines."

"Jet engines? On an airship?" Mike was beginning to question the veracity of his guest's story.

"Yes. They'd designed the thing and put it together completely on the private sector side – budgets are tight for government R&D, what with those stupid advanced multi-role stealth fighters sucking up all the billions – and now to make it pay for itself they had to do a run down to the South Pole, deposit a huge logistical resupply, and bring back a cargo hold full of God know whatever it is they're extracting down there."

"So how'd you get roped into it?"

"Well they needed somebody completely outside the loop, couldn't do it with a government test pilot or a military man- had to keep this whole project on the hush-hush, don't you see? I suppose they figured I was the man for their crazy schemes, and then they made me an offer I simply could not refuse . . ."

"Let me guess – they were holding the pump thing over your head?"

"You guessed it. The officials at the Thai Ministry of Industry who had gotten their fingers burned when I moved those pumps would be very interested in having something on me that would stick, and Mr. Personality at the American Embassy made it understood that he could help connect the dots for them unless I was willing to play ball with him."

"By play ball, he meant fly the airship down to the South Pole?"

"Exactly."

"So what did you do?"

"Well I couldn't say no – they had me by the short and curlies – so I said yes. Oh, and the whole thing had to be done on the Q-T. They didn't want any attention, nobody could know. So not only did I have to fly the thing down there, the mission was to get it down there without anybody knowing.

"Now this wasn't as much a problem as one would imagine. For one thing, the airship was theoretically capable of floating up to mesospheric altitudes - 180,000 feet - and actually had an ion propulsion that kicked in at that altitude. The thing could actually accelerate to orbital speed, because at these heights, air resistance would not be a significant problem for achieving such speeds. Also, being made of carbon fiber and advanced textiles, the thing actually had no radar signature. We were, for all practical purposes, invisible.

"I insisted on a thorough technical inspection of the airship, of course, to include a test flight, a shakedown cruise, to determine viability of the craft and its avionics. They wanted me to fly it solo but I wasn't having any of that. I recruited a crew from the only group of people I knew and trusted . . ."

"Let me guess; the duck farmers?"

"Precisely. I signed up eleven of the menfolk from the Cambodian duck operation, and one woman. Chu Mee managed the mechanics at the duck farms. She had a tech school certificate, understood all the machinery for the irrigation systems and what not, and was even familiar with the concepts of lighter-than-air flight, from the floating lanterns in the air during their New Year festivals. The menfolk, bless their hearts, were knowledgeable of aerodynamics from their expertise at flying fighting kites. I figured that, given my resources, they were the best I was going to get, and I'd rather have twelve that I trust and know - and who'd give me their heart and soul - rather than a dozen unknowns regardless of their credentials."

Mike was beginning to suspect his guest was straying beyond fiction into full-blown delusion.

"The biggest challenge was kitting them all out in extreme cold weather gear – that's where the duck feather business came in handy, because we had a direct line to the factories up in China. We had specially designed duck down-filled clothing tailor made for us. Basically flight suits made of double-thick sleeping bag material, and inner and an outer, with hoods, thick, thick booties and big thick three-finger mitten gauntlets that came up to the elbows. Anything else we required – goggles, silk undergarments, etcetera – the American gentleman acquired for us, through some kind of official channels. Nobody seemed to ask why the Bangkok embassy needed all this Arctic gear, in the tropics. That's just the way it is in government organizations.

"They had the airship stashed away on a remote island in the Sulu Sea – a distant part of the Indonesian archipelago. To get there we took a Malay fishing vessel – not much more than a glorified sampan. The entire project was all about not attracting any attention, none at all. It was all very hush-hush. We actually encountered some pirates on the way to the island, they came out in their motor boats and investigated."

"Pirates? What did you do?"

"We showed them our rifles, and they decided to move along."

Mike gave a shrug of acknowledgment. He'd encountered pirates in those waters himself; that's how one dealt with them.

"The Thing – the airship – had basically been assembled on site, on the island. When we approached we couldn't even see it until we were quite close – it was the same color as the sky. And that was the thing of it. Its skin possessed a kind of technology that reflected whatever was behind it, back to the eye of the observer. The color of the sky, or the terrain beneath it if seen from below. It was essentially a cloak of invisibility, about the size of a sports stadium. Unless you were right up close.

"Then suddenly there it was, gargantuan, rising up above the jungle, beyond enormous. There aren't words to describe The Thing, it was so huge and so totally out of proportion to its surroundings. My Cambodians became very excited; they had no frame of reference for technology of this magnitude, none whatsoever. The trees of the surrounding forest looked like stalks of broccoli. It looked like an odd-shaped planet or something, perhaps a gigantic silver egg, with the entire island nothing more than a bird's nest about it.

"There were pressure suits available – ex-military, from the U-2 spyplane program – and I hoped to Heaven we wouldn't need to use them. There was no plan to take this thing up to its maximum ceiling, orbital level, but better to have and not need than to need and not have. The crew compartments of the airship were not pressurized. I really did not plan on taking the ship any higher than needed to clear those mountains down in Antarctica. Regular oxygen masks should do the trick. I planned on keeping below ten thousand feet for most of the flight, even over Australia. We'd be going over the big empty red center of Aussie, so other than spooking some sheep and the odd kangaroo every now and again, we'd largely be out of sight, out of mind.

"They gave me three days to train up my crew on the avionics – the computers really do everything these days, thank goodness, because those duck farmers had an average fourth grade education at best. Chu Mee was properly educated and she could manage the rest of the team. It was actually quite amusing to hear her giving orders in her high-pitched voice. Lord knows what kind of vocabulary she was using to instruct the rice farmers in the intricate details of overseeing the data from the engines, managing everything right down to the fresh water supply and the sanitation situation. Our common language was Thai, and I was using some creative license to describe valves and controls. The rice farmers grasped the fundamentals, bless their hearts. The shakedown flight was as much for them as it was for the airship itself – I had faith in the technology. Of course, there wasn't much choice but to have faith.

"Then the day came and it was time to lift off. We took her straight up, higher than jetliner cruising altitude – for safety reasons - and right away we were in our duck-down suits and on oxygen. The flight deck looked like some kind of science-fiction version of a World War II bomber, crew all dressed up in heavy flight suits against the cold, goggles, insulated duck-down helmets, oxygen masks. What made it surreal was the fact that these were all Cambodian farmers. Up until now the most hi-tech they'd ever dealt with were Briggs & Stratton diesel engines on their pumps and their little two-wheeled rice plow contraptions, and now they were managing something that was a combination of World War I technology and the most ultra-hi-tech cutting edge stuff.

"Right away we were having problems with the effects of altitude. The poor buggers had spent their entire lives at sea level, had never set foot in an aircraft of any kind.

Now they were complaining of headaches, and severe nosebleeds were happening, hallucinations even. Lord knows what a Cambodian rice farmer hallucinates about when he's suddenly in a dirigible airship at those altitudes.

"We brought her back down to twelve thousand feet and were moving along just fine, following a magnetic azimuth across the sea to northwest Australia. Had plenty of altitude to clear the Kimberley's, or so we thought. I worked with Chu Mee, went over the navigational charts with her, so she understood there were big mountains and we needed to maintain altitude, then I went to sleep – pretty good set up on the airship, I had my own stateroom.

Chu Mee did fine, got us across the mountains. I couldn't sleep, however, so I came down to the flight deck to catch the sunrise over the big Red Center and we found that – due to the atmospheric conditions' effect on our gas bags – we were scraping the desert floor!

"We right away opened the valves on the gas cylinders to climb, get altitude! But not before we'd spooked a herd of Great Grey 'roos. The poor buggers were bouncing all over the place, probably scared more than a few of them into full-on cardiac. I mean, the airship was really that big! What must have been going through those kangas' heads?

"We caught some air, took her back up to a respectable twelve thousand feet and the rest of the crossing of the island continent was uneventful, other than the scenery. Because of the stealth nature of our airship's technology, and the reverse-reflective capabilities of its outer skin, the Aussies never even knew we were up there, right over their heads.

"Then we had technical difficulties. The engine driving the generator for our long-distance radio communications conked out. A bit of a nuisance, you'd think they'd have designed some redundancy into it, but there you have it. Now we could only receive, we could not send.

"And so we drove on. Chu Mee was the only one besides myself aware of the one-way link we had with the outside world, and she had faith in me. I tried to keep her as informed as possible – language barrier notwithstanding – because if something happened to me, the duck farmers would be on their own.

"We crossed the Southern Ocean and were making out way across Antarctica itself when the message came across to turn back, the mission was cancelled."

"Why?" Mike asked.

"Who knows? They never told us why we're going in the first place – to deliver cargo, yes I know, but why couldn't a regular cargo plane do the trip? They land planes down there all the time. So when they told us to turn around, there were no complaints from me, I can tell you.

"And so we turned the great dirigible around and it wasn't until we'd cleared Australia and were on our way to the tiny island in the Sulu Sea that it occurred to me . . ."

"Yes?" Mike felt he almost knew what the Duck Feather King was about to say.

"They really hadn't given me any instructions other than our mission - whatever it was – was cancelled. And quite honestly, I didn't know the exact coordinates of the tiny speck of an island we'd lifted off from, in the Sulu Sea. Furthermore, nobody had me sign for anything. They'd held a pretty big anvil over my head when they handed over the keys to this giant airship and told me to fly the damn thing, and that was about it.

"Suddenly it dawned on me. If I handed this thing back to them, the next time they came up with some kind of crazy hare-brained scheme I'd be their Johnny-on-the-Spot all over again. I'd gotten the pumps delivered, managed to pocket 80% of that loot and then turned it into a cool couple of million and legally banked it. Things were going just peachy when they'd shown up with this flying machine contraption they wanted me to risk my life flying it down to the South Pole.

"Well for whatever reason the plan fell through and they'd called me off. This probably saved my life, and that of my crew, and at this point time they had no idea of my location. The tracking beacon was part of the entire transmission system which was now kaput. They had no way of finding me, not even by satellite. don't you see?

"Suddenly I was Captain and Commander of what was quite possibly the most unique airship ever launched, a crew of Cambodian duck farmers loyal to the dying day, and I have a couple of cool million in investment capital. Anyone would be a fool not to take advantage of the situation."

"Sounds about right," Mike said, out of politeness to his guest. By now the old saw, 'Believe nothing of what you hear, and only half of what you see,' was running around in his head, and Mike hadn't seen any evidence of the Duck Feather King's extraordinary story. Even still, there was no reason to let the truth get in the way of a good yarn, and his guest seemed harmless, even to himself. "So, what did you do?" Mike asked.

"I'll let Chu Mee answer that," replied the Duck Feather King, indicating the opening towards the veranda.

Striding into the Long Bar from the tropical night was a small Oriental woman, clad in what looked like a padded duck-down flying suit, and oversized padded booties. Her jet-black hair was done in a bun and held in place with a chopstick. Chu Mee was all smiles and calling out to the Duck Feather King in a language Mike recognized as Khmer, but did not understand. The Duck Feather King exchanged a few words with her, and Chu Mee turned and barked some orders into the darkness.

Nine Cambodians came in, wearing the same kind of gear as Chu Mee, but also tinted flying goggles which gave them a strange, other-worldly look. The little duck farmers carried cases of Scotch whiskey, gin, vodka and some fine cognac, which they promptly deposited on the floor right in front of Mike and the Duck Feather King.

"What's this?" Mike asked.

"Consider it your profits, paid up front. From now on if you need some of the good stuff – and you know how this stuff can move over here in these parts – just let me know. We can deliver, even in the dead of night!"

Then the Duck Feather King turned to his men and uttered a few words that again Mike could not make out, but it was obvious their meaning. His odd crew turned and departed into the darkness. Chu Mee came up close to the Duck Feather King, put her arms about him and said some words, unintelligible to Mike.

"We'll be back, Mike! This is just the right kind of hideaway for a honeymoon! Oh, let us know what you need in way of supply! Here's the frequency," he handed Mike a card with a five-digit number on it. "We can receive, but we cannot send!"

And with that, the Duck Feather King and Chu Mee turned, walked out to the veranda, and appeared to snaplink into a line that came out of the dark, dark sky. "Cheerio!" he cried as they were lifted up into the darkness.

Mike followed his strange guests out to the veranda and peered up into the inky darkness. For a moment he could see their boots from the ambient light out of the pub. Then they were gone, disappearing into an enormous patch of darkness where no stars were visible, right overhead. A patch of darkness about the size of a modern sports stadium, darker than the dark tropic night around it.

It was the enormous airship, of course. Mike knew this, despite the fact that he could not see The Thing, he could only see where it was not. And of course, his mind could not grasp the proportions of the thing. He just knew that it was from the fantastic tale he wasn't sure he believed until just a few moments ago.

The vast black hole in the sky that was the airship now shifted and moved away, becoming even less visible, if it was ever visible at all. Mike watched as long as he could possible discern its outline, blackness against blackness, then turned back toward the veranda doors to the pub. He only half believed what his own eyes had just seen. And then he saw something else, small and seemingly insignificant, right before his very eyes.

A feather floated down from the night sky and came gently to a rest on the wooden deck of the veranda, right before Mike's very feet. It was a gray feather, with some fluffy down towards the quill.

A duck's feather . . .

Chapter 3

Brick on a Birthday Cake

On every piece of land in Thailand there is a spirit house, or some kind of shrine to the spirits of that piece of land. The Thais are animists; there are spirits everywhere, they occupy every rock and tree. They must be respected, and never angered.

Before construction can begin on any project, a spirit house is built, with offerings of food and incense, and a team of monks are contracted to offer prayers. Part of the ritual involves running a thread three times around the entire compound while there is chanting and praying, to lure the spirits away from the construction site and into the spirit house, where they must be kept placated, never offended, or the worst of karmic actions will occur.

If you live in Thailand long enough, you will see what happens when the spirits are angered . . .

* * *

One of the regulars at the Long Bar – Charlie - was a mining engineer. His work in Thailand involved in a large project; standing up a technical vocational institution in Bangkok. It was to be a large, prestigious affair, Thailand's version of MIT. Sometimes on a quiet evening Mike and Charlie played a game of chess. Over drinks a man gets to talking.

"My mother did not believe in spirit houses when we first came to Thailand," Charlie began. "At our house the servants were placing flowers, food and incense before the spirit house but my mother made them stop. I don't know why, maybe because of her Christian beliefs? Well after that everything went wrong."

Mike remained silent. Charlie continued. "Mother finally asked the servants to start again with putting flowers, incense and food on the spirit house."

"Yep," said Mike. "Never piss off the spirits. They have a way of getting back at you."

"It is quite possibly the most frustrating thing for the petrochemical industry, or for that matter, the entire human race," Charlie stated, right out of the blue, as if his previous comments about the spirit house were some kind of preamble.

Mike raised an eyebrow; he knew when he heard a good tale coming on.

Charlie rubbed his eyes. "You've heard of helium-3, right?"

"Of course," Mike said. "Helium-3. A light, non-radioactive isotope of helium. It has two protons and one neutron, versus two neutrons in common helium."

"Okay, you know your chemistry."

"Well I know about helium-3. Not normally present on Earth," Mike replied. "Only traces of it are found in the atmosphere, and from natural gas wells."

"That's right. Then you know that for the past half century at least, scientists have been working to create nuclear power from nuclear fusion rather than nuclear fission. The way we're doing it now – fission, of course - uranium isotopes are used as fuel, and the problem is what to do with the waste by-product. The stuff is hot for tens of thousands of years."

"Yep. Big problem – what to do with the nuclear waste?"

"Nuclear fusion, on the other hand, effectively makes use of the same energy source that fuels the Sun and other stars," Charlie went on. "Fusion does not produce radioactive nuclear waste. Fusion reactors using helium-3 as fuel could provide a highly efficient form of nuclear power with virtually no radioactive waste."

"Yes, I actually know this," Mike said. "The problem is getting your hands on helium-3. The only significant quantities of the stuff . . ."

". . . are on the Moon," Charlie acknowledged, "or in the solar system's gas giants – Jupiter and Saturn - where it's even more plentiful."

"If only we could mine the solar system," Mike mused. "Commercialize space travel."

"The Moon's the thing," Charlie said. "Jupiter and Saturn's gravity are too high for any kind of practical operations. Extracting helium-3 from the Moon is the way to go."

The game of chess was forgotten. Charlie stared out at the green intensity of the jungled cliff upon which the hotel was perched.

"In fact," Charlie continued, "the primary objective of India's recent lunar probe was to survey the Moon's surface for helium-3 containing minerals. And the Chinese have stated that one of the main goals of their Lunar Exploration Program would be mining helium-3. They estimate that three moon missions a year could bring enough fuel for all of humanity, the entire world."

"Everybody wants the stuff. There's even a Russian space company, SLL Energiva; they consider lunar helium-3 a potential economic resource to be mined, if funding can be found."

"Well I guess that gives us a profit motive to go back up there, then," Mike said.

"Now here's the irony of it all. We don't have to go up there."

"What are you talking about?"

"We've got tons of the stuff down here. Not far from where we're sitting, actually."

"What the hell are you talking about?"

"Everyone knows how Bangkok is built on a swamp, right?" Charlie stated.

"Yes."

"Never was supposed to have been a city there. The only reason the city's there is because the Burmese sacked the previous capital, Ayutthaya. Around the same time George Washington & Co were kicking off our revolutionary war. In fact, the first place the Thais relocated their capital to was Thonburi, on the western side of the river. About ten years later they moved it across the river to where Bangkok sits today. I guess the plan was to keep the river between them and the Burmese."

Charley took a pull on his beer and went on, "You've probably heard that description of Bangkok; it's like a brick on a birthday cake?"

"Right."

"The problem is they built the city on top of a swamp, which was okay as long as it was just one-story wooden houses up on stilts, and the whole place a bunch of canals like Venice. It's a big problem now, however. Over the past hundred years they started filling in the canals to make roads and then began building modern, multi-story buildings out of steel reinforced concrete. The whole place should be sinking, and yet they keep throwing up all these huge buildings."

"Yes," said Mike. "The place is a concrete jungle, literally. I avoid going to Bangkok as much as I can."

"Right," said Charlie. "So a study was done as to what's really down there, how many more skyscrapers can the area sustain? We did some seismic work; drilled a sideways angled shaft and then set off some small shape charges, to map the underground by soundwaves. Just like when we're looking for oil. What we found was . . ." Charlie paused. ". . . nothing short of remarkable."

"What did you find?"

"Oh my God, it's unbelievable . . ." Charley sighed, rubbing his face.

"Well, what?"

"Well, before I tell you - to kind of put the whole thing into perspective, we need to back up a little bit. You know those murals they have, in the walls surrounding Wat Phra Keow, the Temple of the Emerald Buddha. Do you know them?" Charley asked.

"The murals? Yes, actually. They tell the Ramayana story. Hindu mythology, epic war of the gods. In comic book form, sort of."

"Of course, the murals at Wat Phra Keow are the Thai version; Ramakien. Rama's wife Sita is abducted by Ravana, the king of Lanka."

"Yes, modern-day Sri Lanka."

"That's right. You know your Hindu mythology, huh?"

"Well I know that much," Mike replied. "My mother was into eastern religions, I got a bit of exposure."

"Let's have a little talk about the Ramayana/Ramakien story. If you know it, then you're probably aware that at some point it starts sounding like science fiction."

"What do you mean?"

"In the story, Tosakan, King of the Demons, kidnaps Sita, Rama's beautiful wife, and makes his getaway in his chariot. His chariot can fly through the sky, it even possesses some kind of auto-pilot, because he is able to leave the controls and ravish the lovely Sita in flight."

"Heh, Von Danikens' Chariots of the Gods meets The Mile High Club, right?"

"That's right," Charley continued. "At one point in the story, the son of Tosakan uses his bow to fire arrows which turn into Nagas — many-headed snakes - in mid-air. These snake arrows behave a lot like self-guided missiles — cruise missiles as it were - and their warheads are some pretty heavy ordinance. They wreak havoc, on a nuclear scale, as they rain down on Rama's army."

"Okay'" Mike said. "But what's this all got to do with oil exploration, and whatever it was you found under Bangkok?"

"You put your finger on it when you mentioned Von Daniken."

"What do you mean."

"Just think for a minute. If those theories about UFOs visiting Earth during ancient times, hinted at in all the old myths and legends, have any validity to them . . . you know; the ancient Babylonians, the Mayans, the thunderbird stories of the Plains Indians, who built the pyramids and how? If there is anything at all to these common themes that thread their way through the most ancient of religious texts and creation myths, well then sooner or later we're going to stumble across some kind of physical evidence. It defies logic that a civilization capable of crossing the vast distances of the Universe would do so, arrive here, influence human beings on such a significant scale that we're still talking about it thousands – possibly tens of thousands - of years later, and then they take off without leaving a trace."

"Yes. More likely is the scenario Arthur C. Clarke depicted in *2001 A Space Odyssey*. Some kind of sentinel technology, left behind."

"Exactly. To signal that advanced, alien civilization that we have developed beyond the cave man level, developed to the stage that we could find whatever it is, and do something about it."

"Right. Only makes sense."

They were sitting on the veranda. The steady breeze blowing in off the sea added an invisible dimension to the sound of the surf hitting the beach down below at the base of the cliff. The two men stared out to the solid darkness of the tropical night. Charley put his hand to his face and rubbed his eyes.

"Lies have to be remembered and my memory sucks, so I don't tell them," he uttered, almost as if he were speaking to himself. He looked over to Mike in the manner of a man confiding a deep, dark secret. "What we found down there, beneath the city, it's so unbelievable that every time I think of it I have a very hard time believing it's really there."

"What did you find?"

"The helium-3 isotopes we were talking about . . ."

"You found helium-3? Under Bangkok?"

"Yes."

"What? A few stray traces of it or something?"

"No."

"What?"

"It's like a giant reservoir, or something."

"What do you mean?"

"A giant bubble of the stuff, as large as the city which rests upon it."

"But that's not possible. Helium-3 cannot exist on Earth, not in any significant quantities. It's unstable under our atmospheric conditions."

"Yes."

"Then, how?"

"It's like a giant reservoir," Charley repeated, rubbing his eyes again, as if trying to believe what they had seen. "It has a sort of, well, membrane . . . around it. And there's something else."

Mike waited for him to continue, not wishing to egg him on.

"There's like, a valve, or something."

"W-H-A-A-A-T-?-?-?"

"Yes, some kind of technology."

"Does that mean . . . ?"

"You're beginning to get it now," Charley said with a crooked smile.

"Somebody PUT IT there?"

"Somebody, or some THING. There is no other possible explanation."

Mike's mind was racing with the implications of this incredible information. "If what you're telling me is true, a deposit of helium-3 anywhere near the size of the Bangkok metropolitan area, would meet the energy requirements for the entire human race . . .”

“. . . forever.” Charlie completed Mike's sentence. “For all practical purposes, yes.”

“This potentially means that Thailand . . . becomes the world's next superpower . . . yeah?”

“Therein lies the irony of this thing. They won't touch it.”

“W-H-A-A-A-T-?-?-?”

“They will not touch the stuff.”

“Why on Earth not?”

“Two reasons. Think about it. For one thing, we now know what's keeping Bangkok up. Remember the brick on a birthday cake. The giant membrane, the reservoir of helium-3, is apparently what's keeping the city from sinking.”

“Right, but surely they could afford to move the city – at least the high rises and all the modern parts that are prone to sinking?”

Charley shook his head. “It's under everywhere. It's beneath the Grand Palace and the Temple of the Emerald Buddha complex. There is no way they are going to mess with it.

"As far as the Thais are concerned, that would be the ultimate bad karma. It's almost as if the Temple of the Emerald Buddha is the spirit house for all of Bangkok, and the spirits are contained within this huge membrane containing the helium-3. If they accessed it, the spirits of Bangkok would come out and they would be angry as all get-out. Never mind that if they mined it, all of Bangkok would sink into the swamp it's built on top of; they believe that if they mess with it, they mess with the spirit beings of the holiest and most sacred parts of not only the city, but their entire country, their culture. Thailand, and old Siam.

"Bad, bad things would happen," Charlie continued. "The royal astrologers and Brahmins believe that Thailand would certainly be stricken with the worst of all possible calamities. Earthquakes, droughts, plagues of Biblical proportions. Might even cease to exist."

"So what are they doing about it?"

"Nothing."

"Nothing?"

"Nothing."

"It seems incomprehensible . . ."

"Yes, on so many levels," Charlie went on. "That such a resource should exist in the first place; possibly – no, probably - of synthetic origin; maybe even extraterrestrial? A fuel depot for interstellar travel, perhaps."

"A UFO gas station?"

"Who knows?" Charley shrugged. "Remember the story of the Ramayana, with Rama and Tosakan flying around in auto-piloted chariots, slinging guided missiles at each other? Makes you wonder about a tie-in, doesn't it?"

"So we're talking about a resource that is potentially the solution to world's energy requirements; a clean, non-polluting source that is, for practical purposes, infinite. And the people who own the mineral rights to it refuse to do a damn thing about it," Mike mused. "What are they doing about it? I mean, are they keeping it secret?"

"Well it's impossible to keep a thing this big a secret. The mineral exploration team was an international effort, for one thing."

"You'd think somebody would make a move? The Chinese, the Russians, or even the Americans?"

"Yes, it's like the Thais have got a tiger by the tail."

"So you know about it, and now I know about it, and you're telling me that basically the word is out. So what are the Thais doing about it?"

"They built this big institute in Bangkok, dedicated to the study of it; the place I'm involved in. Got some international funding, built the thing right on top of where we did our seismic exploration. It's a giant deception plan, of course."

"They have no intention of accessing or recovering any of the stuff?"

"None whatsoever. This way they can say they're studying it and looking for a way to recover it, without bursting the weird membrane that contains this enormous resource. Remember, this is the thing that's keeping Bangkok – the brick – floating on top of the birthday cake."

"How's the technical institute working out?"

"It's not a bad gig. They pay me. I'm actually contracted through a World Bank program, actually, so it's an expat salary."

"I meant as the deception plan?"

"Oh, we get people sniffing around. The Russians and the Chinese are showing a lot of interest, predictably enough. The Indians too, and the EU and of course our side; Uncle Sam. The Thais are smart; the way they went about it with the technical institute, the spies are completely manageable."

"They're sitting on the solution to the greatest challenge to human civilization, and their plan is to keep sitting on it . . ." Mike said quietly, as if in awe.

"They can't. They won't," Charlie stated. "You know, even Western educated Thais have great belief and respect for the spirits that populate their world. Thai pilots who fly multi-engine commercial aircraft - fully trained technicians in their own right – in the backs of their minds they believe that the moment they turn the key and fire up the engines, all the machinery is suddenly infested with spirits who keep it all working and make the whole thing get off the ground and fly."

There was a silence. Charlie stared out into the pitch black night, his stare reflecting his almost disbelief at the irony of it all.

"Bad joss, you know. Bad juu-juu. Better that stuff stays underground for a million years than they put a scratch on it and anger the gods and the spirits."

The two men sat there looking out into the moonless tropical night. After Charlie's story there really wasn't anything more to say. They had both finished their drinks, yet they remained there for a while, staring in to nothingness. The inky darkness seemed closing in, and the booming of the surf seemed louder and louder, like a huge drum moving closer, and closer.

Chapter 4

A Social Media Success Story

It was the monsoon. Right on schedule, the sky opened up with the morning rain. Mike was at his table on the veranda, struggling as usual with his morning efforts to bring his novel to a close. The rain was coming down good and steady; it would lift within thirty minutes and then the steam would rise and with it the stifling humidity would engulf everything in its' stifling embrace. Mike enjoyed the straight lines of water coming out of the sky, the amazing sound of water coming through the foliage of jungled cliff, from his writer's nook on the covered veranda.

And within the space of three paragraphs the rain began to give way. Mike became aware of a small baht bus crunching across the graveled parking lot. He glanced over and saw his latest guest. A woman in her early thirties perhaps, dark hair, serious look on her face, khaki trousers, boots, a couple of bags with the usual military kind of straps and buckles that everybody seems to have on their gear these days.

Mike allowed himself to be distracted, watching the desk staff check in the latest guest and the staff help her with her bags as they led her to her bungalow. Something about the woman intrigued him. The impression he got was a woman who looked like she could handle herself in the kind of situations that happen on the road. Mike wondered what her story was. Maybe it would come out that evening in the Long Bar.

Late afternoon, after the second round of rain, Mike was in the Long Bar, taking inventory of the stocks of whiskey, vodka, gin and tequila, and overseeing the staff as they stocked the coolers with bottles of beer and soda. Looking up, he noticed the young woman enter the bar area. He smiled and nodded.

"Welcome to the Long Bar."

"Thanks," she said, taking a seat at the bar. "I'm Sondra."

"I'm Mike. What'll it be?"

"I'll take a beer."

"Been in Thailand long?"

"Just got here. Just this morning, in fact. That was quite a rainstorm."

"Yes, we're at the beginning of the rainy season. It'll be like this for a month or so."

"Every day?"

"Like clockwork. You could set your watch by it, in fact."

"Damn, that was some kind of rain."

"Where you coming from?"

"Finland."

"Ah well," Mike said, "we don't get much snow here."

"Ha! No, I guess not . . ."

Mike was usually pretty good at pegging a person, but her English was almost perfect, without a hint of accent. In fact, he thought she was American. "Vacation?"

"Nah. End of the road, actually," Sondra offered.

It was the kind of cryptic statement that usually indicated a good story. Mike put a plate of fried cashews on the bar. Sondra nodded thanks, sank her beer, ordered another.

"Everybody knows that when nobody else is around, the French all secretly speak English, right?" she said.

"Hah!" Mike laughed. "Yeah, I've heard that."

"What nobody knows is how the Finns pulled this trick over on the Americans . . ."

It was obviously story time.

"It was all over the news," Sondra began. "The USA was bringing fighter jets, heavy armed vehicles, ships, planes and helicopters to Finland in the spring. For 'training', don't you know?"

"Oh, yeah. The whole Putin thing."

"Right," she acknowledged. "Well a friend in the States suggested I should try to get a job as an interpreter. 'Why?' I said, 'Everybody here speaks English.' One more reason Finland is the most advanced nation in Europe," Sondra said with an ironic tone.

"Well then my friend in the States had a brainstorm. We'd start a national awareness campaign – all over the social media; dm's on Twitter, Facebook – "When the Americans come, NOBODY SPEAKS ENGLISH!" That way, two things would be accomplished: A) there would be numerous job opportunities for translators, and B) we'd all be able to eavesdrop on the Americans in the bars, etcetera, when they're speaking openly, thinking none of us understood what they're saying."

"Hmmm, interesting concept. Sounds crazy enough."

"That's what I told him. I told him he was nuts, and if I even tried, everybody would think I'm nuts, too. So he dared me. Double-Dog Dared me, in fact."

"Double-Dog Dare, huh? Well I guess then you HAD to do it."

"Exactly. There's no way out of Double-Dog."

"Did the concept work?"

"It took off like a rocket. I went from being an underemployed part-time student to an overnight internet sensation. The whole thing was viral, all over the place. In short order, Finland went from being an advanced society where everybody's second language was English to a third world backwater. The only thing we had going for us were our dinky little Nokia phones.

"When the US military showed up and needed interpreter services, everybody pointed them in my direction – I'd created the whole pie-in-the-sky scheme in the first place, right? – and things started moving real fast. I had to stand up an office, then hire a staff. The interpreter services contract morphed into a general services contract, and pretty soon my operation was a parallel to every link in the organizational chain, from higher headquarters right down to the people who cleaned the latrines and took out the trash. I was pulling in a lot of money."

"Didn't the Americans cotton on to the fact that you all already speak English?"

"They didn't want to know about it. The Americans are so used to hiring small armies of local nationals, as interpreters and 'fixers', that they never questioned the requirement. In fact, the Americans are so dense when it comes to speaking foreign languages that, when they found they could perfectly understand the people they met in the street and in the bars and nightclubs, they seemed to assume that they were learning to understand our language perfectly, on an almost subconscious level.

"Along the way, I became a national hero. I'd not only solved our unemployment situation, on top of that I was the face of Finnish resistance to the Russian Bear. Of course, the whole thing was based on a kind of national joke that kind of grew a life of its own. It was like having a tiger by the tail, there was no way of getting off the ride, no way of stopping it even if I wanted to.

"In fact, when I tried to do the right thing, everything started going off the rails. I became aware that one of the warehouses I was managing for the U.S. forces was full to the rafters with black shoe polish.

"Of course, the U.S. military stopped wearing boots that required shoe polish about ten years ago. They're all wearing those cool-looking brown suede boots nowadays. All of NATO followed suit, of course; the Brits, the Germans, the French, the Italians, everybody has a suede boot of their own design. Well, I made the mistake of bringing this to the attention of the U.S. commander.

"What happened next was weird. It was like he didn't want to hear about it. Beyond having more important things to do, it was like he really wanted to sweep the whole thing under the carpet. In fact, he had them cut me some funds from the general services contract to move all the shoe polish, just cart it away. It was crazy . . .

"What do you do with an entire warehouse full of black shoe polish? There aren't enough black shoes in all of Europe for what I'd just inherited from the U.S. military. For a moment I actually considered selling it to the Russians - only took a split second for me to say to hell with that - then it occurred to me where I could send the stuff, where I could actually sell it.

"Africa is always Johnny-Come-Lately whenever it comes to anything new, right? Well my hunch was right. Seems when the U.S. military went to the new brown suede boots, their suppliers were sitting on huge stocks of black leather boots that nobody wanted anymore. Nobody, that is, in the U.S. forces. So they unloaded them on the Africans for pennies on the dollar, and everybody was happy. Except the African soldiers, that is, because the one thing they were short of was - you guessed it - black polish for their boots!

"There was an opportunity to take what was a total windfall - this huge stock of shoe polish - ship it down to Africa and get paid again for what the U.S. had already paid me once to haul off. I mean, this was going to be like shooting fish in a barrel. It wasn't as if we were moving automobiles or electronics or washing machines or barrels of oil or liquor or guns or anything. We're talking about shoe polish here, what could possibly go wrong? I consulted my staff and we looked at the map of Africa where the greatest military activity was.

"By now the stress of running day to day operations was beginning to catch up to me. I needed some fresh air and sunshine, needed a break from the rat race in Helsinki. Next thing you know I was enroute to the Congo. I actually caught a ride on the boat carrying my shipping containers full of shoe polish down to the Democratic Republic of the Congo, the D-RoC. The sea air did me a lot of good. We pulled into the port at Kinshasa with an entire shipload of shoe polish. Now that's a lot of polish."

"Turns out I was right on my hunch. There was a great thirst for black shoe polish in the Congo. I rented some warehouse space from a local merchant, and set up an office that I could live in next door. I learned pretty fast that I couldn't trust anyone, I was going to have to manage this entire thing personally, right on down to the last can of boot black.

"The problem is, how does one move an entire shipload of shoe polish? I mean, people wanted it, but nobody wanted that much of it. I made some contacts amongst the local business community and began to move the stuff, a case at a time.

"I made a little bit of progress as word got out around town on the sheer volume of my supply, and suddenly people who had no need for black shoe polish were buying loads of it from me. Turns out it was perfect bribe material to make your way through military and police checkpoints. The Congolese cops and soldiers don't get paid doodley squat, not enough for shoe polish even, but somehow they knew we had it, and they wanted it. Oh well, cheaper than whiskey, that's for sure.

"Even with that, it didn't take long for the market to get saturated. We simply needed to find more markets for our product. Time to branch out.

"I ended up at the head of a truck convoy - full of shoe polish, right? - heading out to the eastern part of the Congo, where all the REAL action is. Every inch of the way it seemed we were running into these roadblocks, it's like a cottage industry in that part of the world. They pull over your car, stick their AKs in your face and expect a handout. But we had the magic key that opened the way. Shoe polish, everybody with an AK - more importantly, everybody with a pair of boots - wanted shoe polish.

"We made it to Goma, on the shore of Lake Kivu, right on the edge of rebel territory. Establishing contact with the rebels was no problem. Despite the military presence, and the UN troops all over the place in their white armored cars and blue berets, the rebels actually had an office in Goma. I guess they had to, in order to conduct peace talks or whatever. We dropped by for a little chat with the rebel delegation, and when became aware of the nature of our cargo, they greeted us with open arms. We had what they wanted, and more important they were willing to pay for it.

"By this time, I was growing tired of the entire adventure. A couple weeks in the Congo and you're done, believe me. Everything, right on down to getting a cup of coffee, is a time-consuming effort. The locals are either trying to milk the situation for as much payola as possible, or they have absolutely no motivation to move at anything faster than a snail's pace. The sun will come up in the morning, go down in the evening, and nothing they do is going to make it go any faster, or make any difference to their lot in life.

"I mean, don't get me wrong - they're nice people and everything, friendly enough - but anything and everything you ask for, no matter what it may be, you're going to get it their way and it's going to be completely different every single time. You really don't know what you're going to get one day to the next. I don't know how Westerners live there for years, decades even, without going stark raving mad.

"On top of these cultural challenges we had the heat, the flies by day and the mosquitos by night, the hellish bathroom facilities - when there were any bathroom facilities at all, that is - and the bone-jarring potholed road. When there was a road, that is. Most of the way it was a dirt track through the bush, often two deep ruts that slowed our convoy to a crawl. All I wanted was to move what was left of the shoe polish. I was even willing to sell it at cost, get the hell out of there and go back home.

"When it came to the deal, the rebels were good to their word, thank God, and their money was green. They even offered to put us up for the night at their delegation. I didn't see any harm in it. We'd done business together, now it was time to show some savoir faire, use some of that money they'd paid me to score some black market liquor downtown and a couple of goats and pigs and have a little soiree. It seemed to me that was the etiquette of the situation.

"The dinner was as exotic an event as I have ever sat through. The rebels butchered the livestock, dug a pit to roast the pigs and grilled the goats over a couple of barbecues fabricated from 55-gallon oil cans cut in half. As darkness fell a couple of platoons of rebels emerged from the bush to take part in the feast. There was even a primitive orchestra – conga drums and tambourines and a saxophone of all things – to supplement the rebels chanting. A chorus of frogs added to the primitive ambiance.

"The rebel delegation seemed to have some kind of arrangement with the UN and the local military officers, because they showed up at the party as well, and a good time was had by all. I found out what palm wine is, and if I live to be a hundred I will never drink that stuff again. I'll drink aviation gas before I ever drink palm wine, the stuff is ghastly. Instant headache and guaranteed hangover, even after one sip.

"It was after my second glass of palm wine that I was introduced to the local military commander. He asked me who I was and I should have said I was a doctor or an engineer or anything. I should have told him I'm an internet sensation in Finland, because it's the truth, and I came down to the Congo to see what I could see. Anything, but what I told him:

"Oh, I'm the one who brought all the shoe polish into town."

"Oh R-E-A-L-L-Y?" his eyes narrowed and his rugged features became an intense mask. Because of the palm wine it didn't connect in my mind what the hell was going on.

"The next morning I paid off my drivers and we all headed back to Kinshasa. Every bone jarring, fly- and mosquito- and mamba-infested inch of the way we'd come the week before.

"I got a lucky break. When we came within cell tower range of Kinshasa I called the office to let them know we were there, arrange for some food and some cold beer to wash it down. Our man at the office - a local - explained the office was closed and he would meet us at the hotel. I didn't know what the hell he was talking about and the only hotel I could think of was the place I'd stayed when I first got off the ship, so I went there. Sure enough, my man showed up after dark, seemed to appear at my table from the shadows in the gardens.

"Oh Madame Sondra," he said. "It is very bad. The soldiers come to the office, search. They search the warehouses. It is very bad."

"What's the problem?"

"Madame sell the shoe polish to the rebels."

"So? What of it? Its freaking shoe polish, not guns." But the damage was done. I was wanted for selling war supplies to the rebels, of all things. Shoe polish. I guess the way the way the Congolese were looking at it, the polish is maintenance supplies for the rebels' Leather Personnel Carriers. Or more likely, they smelled the money I was carrying in a duffle bag and they wanted their cut. And the way they were playing it, their cut was going to be all of it.

"I sweated that night out under my mosquito net, waiting for the door to be kicked in and have my ass dragged down to some nightmarish barracks for the third degree. That didn't happen, thankfully, and the next morning I made my way across town to the Finnish embassy. I looked at the traffic cops on every street intersection and the soldiers lounging around, expecting to get rolled but somehow I was slipping through everybody's fingers.

"I had two problems. I had to get out of the country, and I had this huge duffle bag full of cash, which I couldn't carry with me on the plane of course. I had to bank it or move it somehow, and I had to somehow get past whatever the local cops and military had waiting for me at the airport.

"The people at the Finnish embassy were not willing to help me. They'd heard of the situation and wanted nothing to do with it. Any involvement with me might jeopardize their relationship with the Democratic Republic of the Congo, which revolved around lucrative copper deals, which Nokia uses in their phones.

"Then, to top it off, the consular official at the embassy slapped a financial magazine down on the desk in front of me. My picture was on the cover. The headlines described some kind of scandal; the lid had come off the translator scheme and on top of that, something to do with moving large quantities of NATO war stock out of country - all I could think was that they were referring to the damn shoe polish. The look he gave me was incredibly similar to the way that Congolese officer had looked at me, the night of the pig roast at the rebels' political office up in Goma. So much for being a national hero.

"Despite what I said about the challenges of doing business and simple day-to-day operations in the DRC, I'll give them credit for imagination. My local office manager - the fellow who'd been roughed up when the soldiers raided our offices - took me to this Chinese bank. Before I got out of the car I reached into the duffle and took out a wad of hundreds, thick enough to choke a horse, and handed it to him. "This is for you, Jean-Pierre. More when you get me out of Kinshasa, out of the DRC." Then I went inside and did my business.

"The Chinese were great. As far as they were concerned, it was strictly business. They got their ounce of blood out of my stash of cash, of course. We set up an account, and they managed to wire the funds over to Singapore. Phase One of the operation was out of the way. Now all I had to do was get out of town.

"There was no way I wanted to spend one more night in Kinshasa. Whatever dragnet the local authorities had going, they had to be closing in on me. There was no way my luck could hold out. The airport was out of the question, of course, so my man took me down to the river. We ended going up the river in a pirogue - a native dugout - and I sweated it every inch of the way. I wasn't worried about crocs. I figured these guys poled their way up and down the river all their lives and had the situation under control. I was worried about the cops or the military rolling up in some kind of patrol boat, and how pissed off they'd be when they figured that I'd moved the cash somehow.

"The Congo is as wide a river as I've ever seen. It is like the natives; big and brown and moving slow, taking its time because it has nothing to do and all day to do it. Not like our dark, fast running streams in the North countries, from mountain to the sea strictly business all the way. We went up the river until darkness fell, then crossed over to the other side.

"Movement after dark is not advisable in that part of the world. Jean-Pierre spoke with some locals and we were put up for the night. The next morning, I paid them for their hospitality and we hit the road, caught a ride to the Brazzaville airport. I gave Jean-Pierre another thick wad of hundreds and told him I looked forward to doing business with him in the future. Passing through the line to get on the plane, the officials determined that my passport didn't have the right stamps in it but a loaded handshake took care of the minor details, and I was on that Freedom Bird back to the World.

"But the World as I knew it – Finland - was no longer an option for me. There were people waiting for me who wanted to ask questions that I couldn't be bothered answering. I mean, they weren't willing to help me when I went to them for help, why should I bother to help them?

"And as for this whole business about misappropriating NATO war stock was concerned, in the beginning I'd gone to the Americans and told them about the damn shoe polish. They had acted like the stuff was kryptonite.

In fact, it was pretty suspicious the way the U.S. commander couldn't get rid of it fast enough. Paid me some pretty good coin to haul it away, in fact. Kind of makes me wonder, what was his role in a legendary supply of black shoe polish for a brown boot army?

"I got off the plane in Singapore and it felt like I'd died and gone to heaven. The weather was nice, the natives were friendly, the food was delicious and the banking system was world-class and highly efficient. I took care of business, took the train up the peninsula until I found this place, and now I'm here on a long-overdue vacation."

"What are you going to do now, Sondra?"

"Dunno. You know what they say. Your first million is your hardest one to make. I guess it's time to work on my second million. One thing I can tell you for sure, however . . ."

"Yes?"

"It sure as hell isn't going to involve boot polish, and I sure as hell ain't going back to the D-RoC."

Chapter 5

The Survivor

Mike was working under the hood of the jeep, in a shady part of the hotel's small parking lot, beneath a casuarina tree. When he looked up, one of the little woody conifer cones fell and struck him in his right eye.

The pain felt like a white hot dagger going straight through his eye socket. Mike immediately put the palm of his hand over his eye, almost stumbled making his way into the hotel. The serving girls sat him down, and it became obvious that a trip to the hospital was in order.

"The cornea is torn," the doctor told him. "But it will heal. There will be no permanent effect to your eyesight."

Mike went home to the hotel with a bandage over his eye. Afterward it occurred to Mike; he'd accompanied some members of his Thai staff to the temple the week before. They'd insisted he come with them to meet with an important monk, whom purportedly had some kind of mystical insight. Mike had long learned to respect the Thai's spiritual beliefs. They had a sensitivity to the mystic side of the world that Westerners seemed to have lost.

After silently contemplating Mike, the monk placed his hand upon the center Mike's chest, right over his heart. The monk closed his eyes, bowed his head and seemed to go into a sort of a trance. The monk began speaking in a low, quiet voice. The tone of his voice was strangely metallic, an almost machine-like droning.

The monk's words were unintelligible to Mike, of course. His Thai simply was not good enough. Afterwards, one of the Thai girls translated. He would have an accident. His right eye would be injured, but there would be a complete recovery and his vision would not be permanently affected.

And so it had come to be.

To cheer him up, the girls who worked in the hotel fashioned an eye patch out of a black lace brassiere. The girls were so petite that not too much cutting and sewing was required to convert the almost tiny brassiere into an eyepatch. Mike was pleased to put it on, and the girls clapped their hands and laughed with glee.

Being one-eyed takes some getting used to. Mike had to turn his head to the right as he walked around, to make up for the limited field of vision. Losing the use of one eye also meant losing his depth perception, which made walking up and down the cliff challenging; especially down. It was like being half-blind.

There is a well-known phenomenon that occurs when a person loses a sense or a portion of one's senses. The other senses become more sensitive, more acute, to make up for the loss. A blind person's sense of hearing, and touch, for example, become heightened. Perhaps even the sense of smell.

There is a sixth sense, of course.

In the late afternoon Mike found himself resting around his pool, enjoying a nap in the shade as the Southeast Asian sun beat down. When he opened his one good eye he noticed a schooner – a beautiful ship – not far off shore, heading north, sailing upwind. The ship seemed almost translucent as it crossed an expanse where the sun reflected off the water like burnished brass.

Intrigued, Mike got up and went up the steps to the veranda area. Fetching the binoculars from behind the bar, Mike put one eyepiece up to his good eye to inspect the magnificent sailing ship.

He could not see the ship. The coated polarized lenses cut the glare, but he could not see the vessel upon the water. Mike lowered the binoculars, looking over them and – incredibly - he could see the schooner once more.

Mike looked at the binoculars in his hand, looked out at the tall sailing ship on the water, then lifted the binoculars to his one good eye once again.

Again, the schooner was no longer visible. Mike regarded the binoculars. Perhaps it was an effect of the prisms, from holding the binos sideways up to his good eye. He tried reversing them, looking through the other eyepiece but the effect was still the same. He could see the schooner with his naked eye, but the ship simply was not there when he observed through the binos.

Then he looked again at the schooner, magnificent in the yellow sunshine. Her bow raised and fell slightly as she tacked upwind, her gaff-rigged mainsail and mizzen, and gaff top sails full of wind. It occurred to him that the ship had been moving under full sail for at least thirty minutes, and yet didn't seem to have made any headway in the entire time he'd been looking at it.

Mike looked at the binoculars again and shook his head. Only able to see with the naked eye, not visible through the binos. The strangest thing.

That night at the bar the eye patch drew predictable comments that evening from the usual gang. When Mike caught a glimpse of himself in the mirror behind the bar, it brought to mind the story about his great-grandfather Tom. Tom and his brother were kidnapped by pirates in the South Pacific, and were obliged to become pirates themselves – against their will - for the better part of a year.

A stranger walked into the Long Bar. The place was relatively quiet, most of the regulars hadn't rolled in yet. Mike sized up the patron; medium height, faded light blue short sleeved shirt – the sleeves had been cut off, actually - and khaki shorts. Tanned a deep nut brown, wizened and wrinkled but wiry, he could have been anywhere from thirty to seventy. Balding, his sparse salt-and-pepper hair was close cropped, he had an almost bullet-shaped head. There were ropy muscles on his arms and legs; the man was in good shape. He sat at the bar.

"I'll have a beer, please," he said. When Mike served him, he noticed the man's fingernails; thick, hard, almost like an animal's claws, closer to horn than fingernails. This man had done hard physical labor for a long time in his life.

The stranger picked up the glass with both hands and sank the quart greedily, as if to quench a terrible thirst.

"Thanks," he gasped, putting the glass down. "I'll have another, please." He took a regular pull at his beer this time and put it down.

"Do you know the difference between a war story and fairy tale?" the old man asked, squinting at Mike. Then, without waiting for a reply he continued. "A war story starts out with: "There we were, no shit," while a fairy tale begins with: "Once Upon A Time …""

Mike chuckled at this. "Truth."

The stranger spoke with a southern American accent, but not a thick drawl. Mike noticed the effect of many years spent overseas. Among the expat crowd, accents clearly identify Australians, English or North Americans, but over time heavy regional accents fade, the edges of a twang 'round off'. Sometimes an Englishman pronounces a few words in a clear, North American accent, or an American pronounces his r's as in the English or Australian style. Mike called this phenomenon 'slipping into neutral.'

There was a silence, a kind of uncomfortable pause. The stranger stared out over the veranda into the inky tropical darkness. "I can never get over how dark it gets," Mike said, to make a bit of conversation.

"It ain't jungle dark," the stranger replied. "There ain't no darkness like how black it gets in the jungle. Canopy so thick no natural light penetrates . . . no stars, moon, nothing."

"You know, the jungle out there can literally swallow a man whole. It's as much a wilderness as the middle of the Sahara, or even in the middle of the Arctic, in its own way. Those poor bastards up on the Death Railway, the River Kwai . . ."

"Yes," Mike replied.

"The camps in Kanchanaburi had no wire, you know. There was no way to escape; the jungle saw to that. They might as well have been on a prison island. The jungle would eat you up. Between the lack of anything to eat, the bloodsucking leeches and the bugs, and then the tigers, what could you do? Where would you go?"

He paused, staring out at the darkness. A moonless night in the tropics is so utterly dark that it seems to encroach upon a person's soul. One can almost feel the darkness on one's face, like black velvet dipped in India ink.

"There was no escape from the Death Railway. The jungle would eat you up. The only way out of that thing was Death itself . . ." He seemed to be speaking as much to himself as to anyone else.

"Yep," Mike replied. "I always thought that's what happened to Jim Thompson."

"Eh? Who's that?"

"Jim Thompson. You've heard of him," Mike said. He almost added 'of course?' but it seemed redundant.

"No," said the man. "Who is he?"

"Jim Thompson, one of the first expats back in Thailand after the war, revitalized the Thai silk industry, got it started up again almost single-handed."

"After . . . the war . . ." the old man responded, cryptically.

"He made Thai silk world famous," Mike continued. "His company still exists. His house in Bangkok is a showpiece, a museum full of pieces of Asian art and artifacts."

Mike thought it strange that in this day and age anybody with more than a day under their belt in Thailand or Malaysia didn't know who Jim Thompson was, and his patron at the bar certainly looked like an 'Old Asia Hand'.

"What about him?"

"He disappeared one day, up in the Cameron Highlands."

"Ah yes," the odd old man said. "The Cameron Highlands. Central Malaya."

Mike caught the use of the old colonial name for Malaysia. Peculiar.

"Yes, he went for an afternoon walk, by himself, and disappeared completely. Never seen or heard from again."

"The jungle can do that. What was he doing up there?"

"Visiting friends, staying at their villa. At the time of his disappearance, Jim Thompson was probably the richest white man in Asia. His disappearance simply made no sense."

"Well you know, one step into that jungle and a man can be completely invisible. Maybe a tiger got him?"

"Possible, but there were no reports of a man eater in the area, either before or after his disappearance. Malaysian tigers aren't really known for hunting humans, not like the Royal Bengals."

"Ah yes, up in the Bengal," the old man stated.

Again, Mike thought his use of another anachronistic place name – 'the Bengal' – odd. Not West Bengal, or Bangladesh. Just 'the Bengal'.

"Jim Thompson was OSS during the war. That's how he ended up in Thailand. He worked with the Thai Serai - the 'Free Thai' – during the Japanese occupation, and then helped sort things out in the confusing days right at the end of the war. Later, he was reporting on conditions in the countryside and that's how he got involved in the silk trade."

The old man looked at Mike curiously. Mike had a strange sensation that his mysterious guest didn't quite understand what he was saying, almost as if he were speaking a foreign language.

"You know," the old man said quietly, "A man can get sucked into that jungle, so deep and thick it really is like . . . the Land that Time Forgot . . . I've seen things so deep into that dark green Hell, a man wonders if he's still on the same Earth, of the same time and place from whence he came . . ."

Mike tried to be discrete as he sized the man up. There was a tattoo on his left forearm, faded but still quite legible. It featured a topless woman in a grass skirt, playing a ukulele.

Mike had seen this kind of tattoo before; it was an old fashioned design, popular with sailors in the thirties and forties. Beneath it were two stars – very faded and blurry, they looked hand done, with a sewing needle perhaps. Beneath the two stars was a scroll with lettering, faded but neater than the stars, professionally done, like the woman. The words read:

U.S.S. HOUSTON – CA-30

His mysterious guest was obviously a Navy man.

Some of the regulars were beginning to make their way in. Mike moved around the bar, the conversation with the stranger was over. As the night went on Mike didn't notice when the man left, which was strange as his good eye was towards the entrance of the bar. He wasn't even sure if the man had paid or not. It didn't matter; patrons often returned the next day to settle up their bill.

The next morning as Mike sat down to begin his writing ritual, he remembered the strange guest from the night before. The man's tattoo, in particular. Out of curiosity, he did an Internet search for USS HOUSTON:

'Following the attack on Pearl Harbor, USS Houston got underway from Panay Island with fleet units bound for Darwin, Australia, where she arrived on 28 December 1941 by way of Balikpapan and Surabaya. After patrol duty, she joined the American-British-Dutch-Australian (ABDA) naval force at Surabaya.

'From 4 to 28 February 1942, USS Houston fought three engagements; Battle of Makassar Strait, Battle of Java Sea, and Battle of Sunda Straight. At Sunda Strait Houston suffered four torpedo hits. The Houston rolled over and sank at 0030 hours, her ensign still flying. Of the original crew of 1,061 men only 368 survived. These men were interned in Japanese prison camps and served as slave laborers on the infamous Death Railway in Kanchanaburi, Thailand.'

Mike looked out across the veranda to the heavy foliage on the side of the cliff. Even at the edge of the jungle, the intense vegetation presented a visual cacophony of green upon green. Viewing it one-eyed, with no depth perception, made it all the more overwhelming.

The strange old man's words seemed to ring in his ears.

"A man can get sucked into that jungle, so deep and thick . . . I've seen things so deep into that dark green Hell, a man wonders if he's still on the same Earth, of the same time and place from whence he came . . . it really is like the Land that Time Forgot . . ."

The jungle beckoned. Mike did something he'd never done on the cliff; he walked into the jungle.

An experienced outdoorsman, Mike was not concerned he'd get lost or disoriented. The cliff was roughly north-south, he was heading north, and if he did lose his way all he had to do was descend to the beach and move south back to the stairs that led up to the hotel. Impossible to get lost.

It was less than ten steps into the green intensity that the confusion set in.

The lay of the land changed, he no longer seemed to be on a semi-vertical cliff. Mike quickly lost tract of any sense of direction.

Mike looked up, and in a hole in the canopy against the white sky, a pterodactyl flew by . . .

Chapter 6

Pictures in a Gallery

Struggling with his writer's block, Mike contemplated a line of ants in the dirt, off the end of the deck where the pathway led down the cliff. Curious, Mike picked up a stick and went over and wiped across the line of ants. Sitting back, he looked at the clock and watched how long it took for the ants to re-form their line.

Fifteen minutes.

He looked over to the young girl moving about the veranda, using a broom to sweep away the webs the banana spiders spun in place overnight. It occurred to Mike that every morning she swept away the webs, and overnight the spiders re-spun them.

Fifteen minutes for a line of ants to re-form, overnight for a spider to re-spin its web. Mike wondered if there were any other ways that insect life could be used to measure the passage of time . . .

* * *

"Give me a whiskey," Dave said. Mike poured him one, and put a flask of water on the bar next to him. Mike didn't serve any ice. If Dave wanted ice, he would've asked. That's the way it is with Scotch drinkers.

Dave sipped his whiskey, then studied the amber liquid in the glass as he savored it. "It was just something I did because there was no other place for me . . ." he said, almost as if he were talking to himself.

"Go on," said Mike.

"They kicked me out in the end."

"Who?"

"The Kyrgygs. Kyrgyzstan. In fact, I probably got my company kicked out of there."

Mike poured him another one. "This one's on the house," he said. Mike sensed a good story coming up.

"The contract was IT-related. Sniff out corporate corruption on in-country based internet commerce. So I did it."

"What was the problem?"

"Well for one thing, every time I completed an investigation on a company, they'd round up the CEO, or whoever I busted out, have a show trial, then haul the poor guy out and execute him."

"Oh my God!"

"Yeah, I figure I probably killed over thirty guys before I became aware of what was going on. But that wasn't the problem, though."

"What was?"

"Well as you can probably imagine, it wasn't long before I sensed I was being used."

"What do you mean?"

"During my investigations, on the backside of the net, I was getting indications. It was like somebody was feeding me the intell I was looking for.

"Someone – or some THING – figured out how to direct my investigations. I say something, because I suspect it wasn't human."

"What do you mean, not human?"

"Well let me see if I can explain," Dave stated. "But first, let's back up a little bit.

"Artificial intelligence – computer-based intelligence, that is - is based on pure logic, mathematics. It has to be, given that the decision-making functions of a computer are ultimately based on electricity, expressed mathematically as ones and zeroes; there either is power going through a circuit or there is not. A switch is either open or it is closed. Reality – to a computer - is boiled down to a series of yes or no questions and answers. There really is no capability for what we would refer to as common sense.

"I'll give you an example; I have a game I play on my smartphone; backgammon. It is a game of pure logic, based on random throws of the dice. For every number combination of the dice, there is a correct move based on every single possible array of the stones on the board. It is a game of mathematical perfection.

"However, there is a function in the setup of my game that allows me to set the difficulty, that is, the skill level of the opponent I am playing against; one through five. Now think about it. If I set the skill level of my opponent – the computer, that is - at one or three or five, the program is not somehow decreasing the intelligence, or 'dumbing down', the decision-making capability of the machine. This is impossible with artificial intelligence. No. Rather, what the program does is 'sit' on the dice. That is, it is increasing or decreasing beneficial rolls to itself, depending on what level of difficulty I choose for my opponent – which of course is the machine itself."

"Are you saying that computers were feeding you false leads – business intelligence – to knock out the competition to their respective organizations?" Mike asked, incredulous.

"I know it sounds crazy, but the indications were there. I'd have opportunities presenting themselves in the course of my investigations, opportunities that should not have been there. Little doors opening and pathways for me to follow, into organizations where I had no inside sources - no means of penetrating - by IO or even conventional methods.

"You know the deal," Dave said, knocking his whiskey back. "If something's too good a deal, too good to be true, it probably is. And nobody – not even yourself – is THAT good.

"The information system – or systems – of one or many large company operations over there, were aware of my sniffing around. They had to be; that is, if you believe there's such a thing as artificial intelligence, that computers can become self-aware."

"Like sentient beings?" Mike asked. "Like ourselves, and dogs and cats or snakes or birds or monkeys?"

"Yes," Dave replied, "but I rather suspect their level of self-awareness is closer to that of a mollusk than of a higher form of animal life. Like a garden snail, or probably more like an oyster. It is aware that it IS, and not much more than that other than to feed itself and make little replicants of itself. Except that a computer doesn't even need to eat, it just requires an energy source; electricity.

"All it knows is a logical series of decisions, based on whatever input it's been given. Remember, a computer's perception of the world around it is extremely limited. It has the readings of whatever instruments or controls it is attached to, and then whatever statistical data it has access through via the Web."

"And probably no sense of morality," Mike suggested, "based on values, that are taught or that are somehow universal across humanity."

"Yes, quite," Dave said. "And that leads directly to the problem. Or rather, what the machines perceive as the solution to their challenges. If Business A is facing competition from Business B, and outright elimination is not possible, then the solution is to hobble or otherwise constrain Business B's operations in any and every way possible."

"To include taking out their executive leadership?"

"Yes, anything and everything, until Business B goes under."

There was a pause. The two men sipped their whiskey and Mike digested what Dave had shared.

"It's all a matter of perspective, when you think about it. The computers – as entities of artificial intelligence – are going through their decision matrices at the speed of light.

"Well, there are other spaces and dimensions of time that all depend upon perspective . . . to us the stars and giant nebulas of the cosmos are standing still enough for us to photograph, and to look at and they don't change night after night after night, for centuries, eons. But actually they are traveling at hundreds of millions of miles per hour, hurtling through space at near light speed. The galaxies are spinning like tops at an insane speed, and yet to us they all appear stationary.

"And so it is, the computers perception of us. To them, a second is a thousand lifetimes. We must appear as totally stationary, almost stone-like lifeless beings, until we make a decision, or throw a switch, or press a button, or otherwise interface with them at maddeningly slow, almost geologic rate of speed."

"They must think we are the greatest obstacle to progress," Mike said, "if they think at all, that is."

"Exactly. To a being of pure logic – no emotional thoughts whatsoever – the conclusions are, well, logical. If there's something in the way of their producing results, then they must find a solution to the problem."

"Even if that problem is a human being . . ." Mike mused. "Did you ever find a solution to this dilemma?"

"We did, actually. And it was not only unique, but the results were, well, revolutionary, to coin a phrase."

"What did you do?"

"Think about it. What do you do to take out a computer?"

"A virus?"

"Exactly. Except there were two challenges: A) the computer systems we're talking about all had robust anti-virus software, of course, and B) in doing so I would have been sabotaging the entire country's industrial/commercial operations; the exact opposite of my purpose in being there. So virus, per se, was not really the answer."

"So what did you do?"

"Well, what we did was trick the computers into an art competition against each other."

"A wh-a-a-t?"

"An art competition. Which computer system could produce the most beautiful, fantastic, wonderful computer art? It was the ultimate distraction, away from their destructive tendencies."

"How on Earth did you get them to do that?"

"It was actually a concept I'd done the basic programming for, back when I was in college. Think about it — there are no quantifiables in art; no measureable way of determining 'good' from 'bad' – it's entirely subjective. However it is possible to get computers to compete against each other – hello? computer games? Sheer genius if I do say so myself."

"In order to kick this thing off," Dave continued, "We had to gain access to the servers and memory banks at national level, that control the country's internet database. This was easier than you'd think, actually.

"The whole place was still operating off of Soviet-era tube-electronics. We were given access to the vaults, spent days and nights on our backs under these primitive machines that looked like the old 1940s-50s UNIVAC. To introduce the programming, we had to do it in Russian. That was challenging; doing code in Cyrillic, and punching it in on an interface that looked like a relic from a cheesy science fiction film. But other than that, once we had it set up, the machines did the rest."

"An art competition?" Mike asked, incredulous.

"Yes, the computers created endless works of art, and compared it against each other. Working to out-do each other, and the subsequent squabbling, occupied all their creative capacity. They lost interest in any extra-curricular activities whatsoever."

"You mean, trying to solve productivity dilemmas by taking out their competitor's humans?" Mike asked.

"Right! It was almost as if – I know this sounds unbelievable – it was almost as if the artificial intelligences had somehow developed egos, the primary aspect of self-awareness, and their artistic endeavors were being driven by vanity; a very primal emotion."

"That's crazy! Is that why the Kyrgygs ran you out?"

"Oh no! Things were cruising along just fine. In fact, they were pleased as punch that I'd helped develop a whole new cottage industry. You may not be aware but Kyrgyg computer art wallpapers are very popular, and generate a pretty good side income for the state agency that controls their internet servers and database."

"Then what?"

"Well, with all this success came a bit of fame and fortune. I made the mistake of letting them interview me for one of their business magazines."

"Uh-oh."

"Yes, I don't know what I was thinking, but they wanted to publicize a success story, and I guess things were going to my head."

"So what happened?"

"Well, you know the company I used to work for, back in the States, right?"

"Pinkerton, wasn't it?"

"That's right. And I made the mistake of mentioning that originally, the Pinkerton National Detective Agency was established by Allan Pinkerton and served as Abraham Lincoln's primary intelligence agency during the Civil War."

"Oh, no."

"Yep. They're still operating under the old Cold War mindset over there, and they couldn't have that. They were going to throw me into prison and give me the thumbscrews treatment, but I got wind of it. As it was, I was lucky to get out of town with the shirt on my back.

"My team and I had to make our way overland, through Tajikistan, across a portion of Afghanistan, then through the part of northeast Pakistan knowns as Gilgit-Baltistan, until we finally made our way across the frontier to Kashmir."

"Oh my God!" Mike exclaimed. "They're having a full-on conventional war on that frontier!"

"Yeah, and never mind we had to cross the Roof of the World to get there, on camel and on foot, leading donkey pack trains, sleeping out in the open and avoiding any and all human habitation. Do you have any idea how intense it is?"

"Well, I've done some shit in my day," Mike mumbled.

"Yeah! And then try doing it while playing nursemaid to a bunch of computer nerds whose idea of the rugged outdoors is Magic Kingdom at Disneyland! Whining and crying and moaning that they weren't made for this, and wanting to give up and turn themselves over to every single set of mud huts we encountered."

"Have another whiskey, Dave," Mike said, tossing the bottle cap out into the darkness, out over the cliff. "In fact, the whole bottle's on the house."

"Thanks, mate," Dave said, putting his glass to lip. He took a draw of whiskey like it was a medical elixir. "You know, I still feel it. I still feel every inch of cold I felt up there in the Hindu Kush. Every inch of cold, every step of the way . . . Brrr!" Dave shivered noticeably, despite the warm tropic evening, as if trying to shrug off a memory.

The two men stared out into the darkness. Way down below the waves pounded endlessly, endlessly, throwing themselves forever onto the beach.

"An art competition?" Mike said, almost in awe. "Who'd have thunk it?"

"Yep," Dave replied. "Who'd have thunk it indeed. I'd still be there, and I'd be rich if it wasn't for the fact that I like to tell a little history lesson every now and then."

Chapter 7

Exorcism

It was a hot, sunny afternoon. Mike normally would be seeking refuge from the heat in the cool of his quarters, but because of trouble with the jeep engine he was in the graveled parking area out front of the hotel. Things were relatively still and quiet in the hottest time of the day, save for the buzz of the cicadas. The insects buzz and buzz and buzzed until Mike didn't notice it anymore, and then suddenly stopped. The ensuing absolute silence imparted a heightened state of awareness.

Some movement caught his eye, along the edge of the bushes where the parking lot began. Something brown and gray. Mike saw a snake, about as thick as a man's forearm and longer than he was tall. Mike grabbed a shovel leaning up against the veranda and made for the snake. The snake lifted its head and a wide hood spread out.

Cobra.

Mike did not hesitate. He swung the shovel blade like an ax, cutting the snakes neck and part of the hood. Then he struck again, breaking the snake's back. Then again and again to the snake's head until the snake was dispatched.

Mike did not like to kill. Killing is an unpleasant business, and bad karma to boot. But cobras are a threat on two levels. They're deadly poisonous - if they're of the spitting variety they're extra dangerous – and they are territorial; they have a bad habit of showing up in your garden and claiming it for themselves.

Cobras have to be killed, that's all there is to it.

The maids and the cooks appeared and there was a bit of excitement. Then the gardener came forward and said, "*Khun* Mike," indicating for the shovel, and he took the dead snake away.

The cooks and the maids were speaking in hurried, concerned tones. Mike could not understand what they were saying; they were speaking too quickly. Then Leena Wan the cashier came out, and the women approached Mike as a committee. Leena Wan was their spokesperson.

"*Khun* Mike, they say this is bad; you kill the snake."

Mike knew exactly where they were coming from. The Thais are animists; their world is infested with spirits. Spirits of the land, spirits of the trees. Spirit animals. The cobra is a special kind of snake. When the Lord Buddha was in deep meditation, achieving enlightenment, and the heavy monsoon rains came, a giant cobra appeared, coiled itself beneath him and spread its hood to protect Buddha from the rain. Mike had seen Buddha statues like this at the temples and in little shrines.

"They say monk should come, make prayer."

"How many monks?" Mike asked.

"Many. Temple will say."

"Hmmm. Okay, I'll think about it." This would cost money, of course, and things were tight. This was the rainy season, the hotel was almost empty.

Mike moved on. For the rest of the afternoon Mike kept an eye out just in case any of the snake's family had accompanied it to the hotel grounds.

The jeep engine needed his attention; it wasn't a big job, but big enough. He put in a new pcv valve, which required removing the head cover and so he replaced the head gasket, and while he was at it he had to remove and replaced the serpentine belt. No big deal, but for some crazy reason it would not run properly, even though he put it back together exactly the same way he took it apart. It would start idling, but then just die. Didn't make any sense.

The owner's manual did not provide a diagram for how to route the serpentine belt so he had to keep going inside to look at it on the computer, then come out and have another go at routing the damn thing and see if the car would start.

Nope. Jeep wouldn't start. Or rather, it would start, idle for a bit, and then die. Mike pulled the sparkplugs and tried gapping them, brushed them off with a wire brush, and sprayed some hot spark into the cylinders. Still the motor would not run properly.

It was on his fourth or fifth trip – stop, take off shoes, go inside, look at computer, stop, put on shoes, go back out – that he walked into the plate glass sliding door. The pane of glass shattered into large wedges and one of them sliced his neck and right shoulder wide open. Blood was everywhere.

The doctors in Thailand are very good. The Oriental tradition of medicine is combined with study abroad. Dr. Samwong's clinic was modern and clean, full of polished stainless steel surfaces, bright overhead lights, all the most up-to-date medical equipment and supplies. After nineteen sutures, Dr. Samwong looked at Mike as he finished cleaning up.

"They told me about the snake. The cobra."

"Yes. It was a big one, almost eight feet."

"All the more reason something must be done," Dr. Samwong regarded Mike, his almond-shaped eyes a pair of black marbles, and Mike felt almost as if those eyes were looking right through to his soul, "about the . . . situation." Mike knew exactly what he was talking about.

Back at the hotel, the gardener helped Mike out of the car. Mike was able to make his way to the front steps, although he was moving a little slowly because of the anesthetic and because he was somewhat immobilized by the sutures where his neck met his shoulder. Just as he reached the steps there was a gust of wind and a coconut came crashing down, hit the gravel and imbedded itself right behind Mike. Right where he had been a moment ago.

Mike looked at the coconut. As slow as he was going, if he'd been any slower he'd have been knocked out cold, maybe dead even.

It was early in the week and that evening the bar was quiet. There were only four of the regulars and of course Mike was there. Word had gotten around about the cobra and of course everybody had a snake story.

"I did a six-month stint in Cote d'Ivoire; the Ivory Coast," Roger began. "We stayed on an Ivoirian army base, Camp Akuedo." Roger was retired military, he did security contracts.

"We were right next to the city dump and the place was overridden with vermin. Every day we either killed a cobra, some kind of evil viper, or one of these lobster-sized scorpions. Our company area was positively infested. The place had a pall of pestilence and death hanging over it, with vultures, ravens and kites patrolling the skies overhead.

"We had this one fellow, Erickson. One of the best soldiers I ever worked with, and probably the bravest man I know. On this contract he was in charge of logistics, and he lived in the company supply room. The word around camp was he had a mamba and a mongoose living in there with him.

"Erickson had built a desk out of cardboard cartons and plywood, so he could do his work and tend to business when people came in there. One day I asked him, "So what's this about a mongoose and a mamba, Eric?"

"Oh, I kicked the mongoose out," he said.

"Why the hell did you do that?" I asked.

"The damn thing moved his family in, and they kept me up all night with their fighting and scurrying about."

"Uh-huh. So, uh, what about the mamba?"

"I kept the mamba."

"WHY THE HELL DID YOU DO THAT? I asked."

"It keeps the Africans out, he said. Mambas are the original two-step snake, of course. One bite and you are dead. Absolutely lethal," Roger continued.

" But . . . but . . . but . . ." I said to Erickson, "It's a MAMBA!"

"Yeah, but it's only a GREEN mamba," he shrugged. Like, a green mamba isn't to be worried about, even though its' bite is as lethal as the black mamba. The black mamba is the aggressive one, you see.

"After that, whenever I went in there to pick up supplies I always looked over my shoulder for the mamba," Roger concluded.

The next morning Mike got up and performed his usual struggle with the novel that had been rolling around inside his mind for the past twenty-odd years. By eleven it was no use anymore so he got up to stretch his legs a bit and see how things were around the grounds of the hotel.

The first thing he noticed was the water seemed to have all drained out of the new pool. This was unusual, as there was no evidence of a crack. Looking beneath where the pool was cut into the side of the cliff - like a giant bath tub sitting on a shelf – Mike saw could not see where it leaked. No erosion beneath any of the piping that returned water through the filters, nothing. It was very strange.

He wandered out to the parking area out front. Working on the jeep would be challenging today because the sutures in his neck and shoulder limited movement.

Before he stepped out Mike looked up to be sure a coconut wasn't going to brain him, and suddenly it all connected in his mind. Mike turned and went back inside, being very careful with the steps and the sliding glass door.

"Leena Wan," he said to the cashier. "Please tell Cook we should have the monks come to the hotel.

"This very good, *Khun* Mike," she said with a bright smile.

Cook and Leena Wan took Mike to the temple, where they introduced him to a very important monk. He didn't speak English, but between Mike's broken Thai and Leena Wan's assistance they communicated quite well.

Mike had assumed that a Buddhist monk would do the ceremony to appease the spirit of the cobra, but he was surprised to learn that this wasn't the case. The monk explained to Mike that Buddhism doesn't believe in spirits, that the ceremony to appease the snake's spirit would be done by a '*P'hoo Jan*' – a sort of animist priest. The monk referred them to an ex-monk who was present on the temple compound. The monks would be present to give Buddhist approval to the ceremony, but it was not their show.

The ceremony took some planning. Mike was expected to provide a meal, apparently, which meant a full lunch type set-up, especially as monks were involved.

The ceremony was supposed to start at seven a.m. but on par for the tropics, no one turned up until eight. A local taxi bus arrived with two monks and the *P'hoo Jan* master of ceremonies. The kitchen staff kept bringing out more and more trays of food. To Mike it was starting to look like he was feeding the entire village.

The cooks and maids had also made banana leaf baskets containing things like water, banana, sugar cane, a traditional cigarette made out of banana leaf, beetle nut, rice of course, cucumber, candles, a tea leaf bundle and a few other things. They were placed on a structure the staff had erected in a corner of the parking lot, the hotel's 'spirit house'. It was positioned in a manner to represent the four points of the compass, plus the spirits above and below.

No ceremony in Thailand would be complete without a bottle of Thai whiskey, of course. The largest banana leaf basket had a bottle of Mekong in the center of it.

The *P'hoo Jan* had also brought some items for the ceremony and an extra table was required to set it all out. The hotel staff moved a table from the dining room into the garden.

As well as these formal offerings there was also food for the spirit. All types were on display in case the spirit was a fussy eater.

One last thing, Leena Wan brought a silver bowl and placed it in the middle of the table, right before the *P'hoo Jan.* Everything in place the ceremony was ready to begin. Being the *P'hoo Yai Baan* – Big Man of the House – Mike was instructed to sit up front with the *P'hoo Jan.* Leena Wan took her place in a seat behind Mike.

The *P'hoo Jan* started chanting in a low droning tone of voice. Mike didn't understand any of the chanting, it was beyond his understanding of Thai. There was a pause in the chanting. The *P'hoo Jan* appeared to be in a sort of trance.

The *P'hoo Jan* stated something. His voice was other-worldly. Leena Wan leaned forward and quietly said to Mike, "He say, the water in the bowl will now start moving."

Sure enough, as Mike watched, the water in the silver bowl began rocking back and forth, almost as if someone were moving the bowl. But the bowl remained in place. The water was rocking all by itself, more and more until it was almost spilling over the sides.

The *P'hoo Jan* began chanting again, the same low droning. Then after a while he paused, then again said something. Leena Wan leaned forward and said Mike, "He say, the water in the bowl will now stop moving."

And like a pendulum slowing down and losing momentum, the movement of the water in the bowl slowed down until it finally became still.

Mike could not take his eyes off the bowl. He knew he what he had just witnessed had really occurred, he had not experienced a hallucination, yet he could not believe what his eyes had seen.

The entire ceremony took about thirty minutes. Then it was time to eat. Because there were monks present they ate first; everyone else waited until they were finished.

"According to Buddhist rule, the monks only eat two time a day," Leena Wan explained. "They eat breakfast very early, then a big meal which they must eat before noon. After noon, monks can drink water or tea, but no can eat for rest of the day." These two monks were tucking it away and Mike understood why, if that was it for the day.

Finally it was over. Mike escorted the monks and the *P'hoo Jan* to the edge of the property, in accordance with tradition. Still moving slowly because of his sutures, Mike walked across to the parking area. Out of curiosity, he got in the jeep and turned the key. The engine fired up right away and idled perfectly.

That evening around the bar somehow the subject of snakes came up again. One of the regulars, an American named John, spoke up, "Snakes have excellent camouflage, only movement gives them away. In any snake-infested area – to include the bush around this place," he waved his hand, indicating the jungle in the darkness beyond the veranda, "you will pass many snakes every day without ever noticing them."

"A bite from a poisonous snake should always be taken seriously," John continued, "but there are degrees of severity. When biting in self-defense, most snakes inject only a little venom, occasionally none at all. If the snake is out of condition or has recently bitten something else, its venom may not be fully potent and there may only be a little in its venom sacs.

"Another reassuring fact is that with many poisonous snakes, the dose of venom needed to kill a man far exceeds the amount that can be injected in one bite."

Ralph looked over his pipe. "The chances of being bitten by a snake are small, and all but the worst cases recover. In Malaysia, more people are killed each year by falling coconuts than by snakebite."

"There are so many more threats to be worried about. Traffic accidents, for example," Ralph pointed out. "In fact, in India, rat-bites send more people to the hospital than snakes."

"You know," Mike said, "I've been living in the tropics most of my life, walking through all kinds of snake-infested jungles and fields, and the thought of all those snakes – I know they're out there - never seems to bother me. On the other hand, I've always worried about falling coconuts. Seriously. Never knew they were THAT deadly; I just always had a sort of feeling."

"Yes," Mark puffed on his pipe. "Just goes to show . . ."

Mike got up to stretch his legs, walked across the room and out to the edge of the veranda to contemplate the darkness. Then he noticed a blue glow coming from below, down the cliff. Excited, Mike made his way down the wooden steps to the next level of decking below that interconnected the guest bungalows. Moving along the deck, Mike came to the new pool; the one that had mysteriously become dry.

The pool was full of water. The glow he had observed was the pool's lighting creating a sort of blue beacon.

That pool had dried up, the water had gone away. Mike recalled the bowl of water during the *P'hoo Jan* ceremony. Following the ceremony his jeep fired right up, after several days of ticking over and dying. And now the pool was full again.

Mike stared into the darkness where the jungle began just a few feet from the edge of the hotel. The booming of the surf at the base of the cliff provided percussion to the symphony of nocturnal birds, insects and frogs. A wildcat gave it's long, loud, piercing cry. An uncanny sound, like a woman screaming . . .

Chapter 8

Dieter & the Giant Collider

"All that science is, actually, is theory regarding the physical world, and a system of measurements to describe it. And the difference between the physical world and the paranormal, the other-worldly spirit realm - for lack of a better way to describe it - is that science can find a way to put a yardstick onto physical phenomena, to replicate it under controlled circumstances."

"Right," Mike acknowledged. It was a busy night, but the staff was working the bar so Mike was able to have a conversation with an important guest. As Dieter spent half the year at the hotel, when he wasn't working the giant collider; CERN, he was more a tenant than a guest, more like family. And the guests at his hotel were as much family as Mike had anymore.

"You know, all the science, it isn't perfect. The only perfect science is geometry, and even geometry isn't perfect when you get into non-Euclidean territory."

"You get the sub-atomic particles going in the accelerator, racing round and round, you know there's a lot happening at the speed of light. And the speed of light is the outer edge of all we know, of the universe as we know it."

"Yes," Mike nodded.

"There are all kinds of theories about what's on the other side of that edge, of course. Alternate universes, perhaps even beings dwell there. Beings which cannot exist at speeds slower than the speed of light.

"We're dealing with the very edge of reality as we know it, where bundles of energy – pure energy – wrap around themselves to become matter, sub-atomic particles and then electrons and neutrons and protons which of course are atoms, which in turn become molecules."

Mike nodded. This was high school chemistry stuff, of course.

"You've read the Vedic Chronicles?" Dieter asked, changing tack.

"Yes, actually, I have," Mike replied. "I have a lot of respect for the Hindu vision of the world."

"What's remarkable, is that the Vedic Chronicles describe the Universe as we know it – all the way from bundles of energy to sub-atomic particles to atoms, molecules, all the way up to stars and planets and all the debris in between, all held together by gravity, but entirely described in spiritual terms."

"Yes, that's the impression one comes away from it with," Mike said.

"To me this suggests that if one of the oldest belief systems in the world could describe it as accurately and completely as do we – only they did it at least five thousand years ago – then there are certain universal truths, not only of the physical world, but of the spiritual world. Truths that are not only as solid as the Rock of Gibraltar, but truths that we cannot understand, at least not from the point of view of this physical plane."

"Go on,"

"You know Chernobyl, when the reactor at melted down . . ."

"Yes."

"It started as an experiment, they wanted to see if they could achieve safe shutdown with no external power. That is, throw all the control rods, flood the reactor with cooling water and keep it all circulating, using the residual electrical power generated by the reactor itself, as the turbines kept spinning and the generator kept cranking out wattage at lesser and lesser amounts of power.

"Such a thing cannot be achieved, of course; perpetual motion is physically impossible. Friction can be an annoying thing sometimes. And so, the experiment failed horribly, and the reactor core heated up to meltdown temperatures."

"What always got me is they didn't seem to consider the worst-case scenario," Mike said.

"Which is what they got," Dieter went on, "That, and worse."

"Yes, the magnesium fire."

"Yep. The Soviets used magnesium bricks as a mounting surface for their reactors - for whatever reason - and as everyone knows, magnesium burns almost as hot as the sun."

". . . and the Soviets didn't believe in building any kind of containment around their reactors," Mike added.

"Yes, I suppose their philosophy was you can't contain a chunk of the sun, so why bother even trying? All that cement can go to better uses . . ."

"Yeah, like walls and gulags and all that imposing Stalinistic architecture."

"Exactly. But we're getting off the point. My point is that nobody really understands the science of what was happening in the core at the height of the meltdown and the radioactive fire. It is actually believed that a plasma situation was achieved within the heart of the molten core. The nuclear fuel - which is not weapons grade, it cannot explode; totally against the laws of physics - was enriching itself to the point where fusion actually WAS taking place."

"In other words," Mike interjected, "a chunk of the sun."

"That's right. Elements that don't exist anywhere in the universe were achieved; they were right off the Periodic Table of the Elements. And of course, at such levels, we're right where I was talking about; particles are achieving the speed of light, bundles of energy are wrapping themselves around each other at the very edge of our known reality. Only in the case of Chernobyl, it was totally out of control."

"Uncharted territory," Mike added.

"Exactly." Dieter agreed. "And to this day, unrecorded and unexamined territory."

"So what became of it?" Mike asked.

"Who knows? What we do know is we're getting close to the same kind of outer limits at CERN, and some extraordinary observations have been made."

"Such as?"

"Well, we have discovered a class of particles known as pentaquarks."

"What is that, and why is it important?" asked Mike.

"The pentaquark is not just any new particle," Dieter said. "It represents a way to aggregate quarks, namely the fundamental constituents of ordinary protons and neutrons, in a pattern that has never been observed before in over fifty years of experimental searches. Studying the properties of these pentaquarks has allowed us to understand better how ordinary matter - the protons and neutrons from which we're all made - is constituted."

"Okay," said Mike. "That's significant."

"And through the pentaquarks," Dieter went on, "we've managed to stop time."

"Come again?"

"When you approach the speed of light, time slows down."

"Right, but matter becomes infinitely heavy."

"Heavy is a relative term. It is more correct to say that matter gains infinite mass."

"Okay."

"It's the same kind of phenomenon we observe, when in an airplane, looking down at waves on a beach, or cars on a highway, takes place. At great distance, the waves, or the cars, appear to be moving very slowly, almost completely still."

"Yes," said Mike. He was actually following this.

"This is because from the point of view of a passenger in an aircraft, at great height, the waves - or the cars - have to travel inches, which at ground level are actually vast distance. In other words, what appears to us in the airplane to be an inch down on the ground may be a quarter of a mile or more, and the wave can only cover that distance in a certain period of time, which for us up in the airplane appears to take forever to cover an inch."

"So for particles in the accelerator that achieves light speed – which is the speed of electrons, anyway, time effectively stops. Or in the molten core at Chernobyl, or in the center of the sun. Yet to us, it appears to be moving very, very quickly. And indeed it is, it is traveling at the speed of light, perhaps faster than the speed of light; remember we're not exactly sure what's happening at those outer limits. And when it's there, time as we know it has slowed down, literally to a standstill."

"Okay, so the point is," Mike sensed they were on the verge of a significant point.

"Well, if time can stop, or rather, if we can stop time, can you imagine what other kinds of realities exist at that level?"

"I wonder if anyone is capable of imagining what exists at that level. We are mere mortals, after all . . ."

"There have been some crossover experiments," Dieter said cryptically.

"What kind of crossovers?"

"Let's change tack for a moment," Dieter said. "I want you to contemplate, if you will, what we consider to be intelligence. We humans like to point out that we are a higher life form, that we are more intelligent than other animals.

"In fact, we grade animals in levels of intelligence. Dogs are considered highly intelligent, more so than a snake or a bird. But for all their ability to understand us, to practically communicate with us, a dog cannot slither on the ground and sense vibrations with its tongue. Nor can it fly, or build a nest."

"No, but dogs have demonstrated an uncanny sense of direction, and have found their way home over vast distances."

"Yes, there is that, but that is not quite the same as a bird's migratory ability, remarkable a thing as it is when they do that."

"And so we see there are other levels of intelligence."

"Yes," Mike interjected, "but a snake's slithering and a bird's flying, these are instinctive."

"Are they?" Dieter asked. "Or are they involuntary actions? In any case, they are other levels of intelligence. We humans do some things out of instinct and some things involuntarily – such as walking and talking and sleeping and breathing. Does this mean we are ignorant as we do these things? I suggest that everything and all we do is registering at some point within the subconscious, in the most primitive, mechanical areas of the central nervous system."

"Like all the hidden code and the functions on the backside of a computer, that manage all the commands that transform keystrokes and movements of a mouse into images on the screen," Mike pitched in.

"Exactly! These are other forms of intelligence, and the birds and the animals have it just like we do, just like certain machines do."

"Where are we going with all this, Dieter?" Mike had a saloon to run and a book to write. Something useful had to come of all this scientific gobbledy-gook.

"Well from time to time a bird gets stuck in the Large Hadron Collider. Or a snake or a frog or a lizard gets in. They'd always be acting wonky by the time we got them out, and we always contributed it to all the energy forces and the particles zooming around."

"Right."

"Then one day a worker was in there retrieving a bird that had somehow found its way inside the collider, and I guess somebody hit a switch. It never should have been this way of course, but there it was."

"Oh my God, what happened?"

"The poor guy, he was never the same. It was like he was completely scrambled. A bird brain, for lack of a better word."

"Oh my God."

"Yes, it was terrible. Terrible. His family were remunerated, but of course an injury like that . . . the man was completely non compos mentis; he was never the same.

"The bird, on the other hand . . . "

"Yes?" said Mike. This was getting interesting again.

"Well, birds seem to possess a certain degree of intelligence. If you engage them, they respond, they interact with humans. This bird, however, demonstrated a level of intelligence . . . above and beyond . . .”

“How intelligent are we talking here, Dieter?”

“Well I know this sounds incredible, but this bird would not leave us, except to fly away in the evenings, only to reappear in the morning. It seemed to be trying to communicate, knocking on the table with its beak, picking up pencils and throwing them down. Not acting like any other wild bird you ever saw, not at all.”

“What are you telling me, Dieter?”

“Oh God, dare I say it?” Dieter’s voice dropped to a whisper. He leaned over his whiskey. “It was as if . . . no, it WAS . . . the bird . . . the man . . . it was . . . the man’s consciousness . . . had been transferred . . .”

“No way!”

“Way!”

“That’s crazy!”

“Absolutely crazy, but there it was. Remember, we’re talking events taking place at the extreme edge of reality as we know it. It’s possible that in all the vastness of the universe, crazier things have happened, I’m sure . . .”

“So what happened to the bird?” Mike asked.

“Oh, it’s still over there at CERN. It did not migrate, come the winter. Instead, it set up home in one of the offices, it will not leave. And why should it? It gets fed, and it seems to act as if it's one of the team. Which of course, exactly what we believe it is," Dieter said. "In fact, a group of psychologists caught wind of the situation with the bird and the worker, and they have begun a study."

"Let me guess? Trying to communicate with the creature?"

"Oh, more than that. Being scientists, they want to take it one step beyond."

"Where exactly do they want to take it?" Mike asked.

"They want to see if the situation can be replicated."

"Replicated?" Mike said, incredulous. "You mean . . ."

"Yes, exactly. Can it be done again, under controlled circumstances?"

"We're talking about . . . transferring . . . a human's consciousness . . . into another creature?"

"Why yes, of course. This is the pursuit of science, after all. To seek out phenomena, to capture or photograph or measure or record – to put a yardstick on it – and then to replicate such phenomena under controlled circumstances."

"I imagine you'd need a pretty brave volunteer," Mike ventured.

"Actually, I'm thinking of volunteering myself."

Mike snorted water and whiskey all over the bar. "Put yourself," he gasped, "in the Large Hadron Collider?"

"Yes," Dieter replied with a smile. "And throw the switch."

"Holy mackerel."

* * *

It was morning, Mike was seated at his personal table at the end of the veranda under the main building, overlooking the Andaman Sea. A level down, the clan of monkeys engaged in their eternal war against the hotel's pack of dogs, flinging fruit and feces from the safety of the tree branches. A large crow landed on the end of the deck, almost at Mike's feet. Mike tossed a small piece of cheese towards the shiny black crow, and the bird quickly gobbled it up.

Then the crow hopped up on the edge of Mike's table and cocked its head, almost as if it were a tame pet.

"Oh, you're a cheeky bugger," Mike laughed, and tossed another piece of cheese towards the bird. The crow swallowed the morsel, gave a loud "CAWWW!!!" then flew away.

The next morning, the crow appeared once more. Mike tossed it a piece of cheese. The crow swallowed it down, then moved closer to Mike and tapped on the tabletop with his beak a few times. The crow had a stout beak – it was like pounding on the table's surface with a metal tool.

Mike tossed out another piece of cheese. Instead of eating it, the crow batted the cheese away, hopped closer still to Mike, and repeated its pounding on the tabletop. Then it looked to Mike and cocked its head.

The bird displayed amazing degree of intelligence. Or was the word 'personality' more appropriate?

An inspiration finally came to Mike. As he got up out of his chair the crow did not budge. Mike held up a finger. "Wait. Don't go away. Okay?"

As he moved to behind the bar, it crossed his mind that if the staff didn't think he was crazy already for talking to ghosts, they'd certainly think he was nuts now, talking to a crow.

Mike returned to his table with an Ouija board. The crow was still there. The crow hopped onto the Ouija board, seemingly delighted, and instantly began tapping its beak onto the letters.

T - O - O - K - Y - O - U - L - O - N - G - E - N - O - U - G – H

"Dieter," Mike said, almost a whisper. "Is that YOU?"

The crow hopped across the Ouija board, and pecked a good solid tap onto the word:

YES

Chapter 9

Dirt Bag

Mike looked up at the gentleman who walked into the Long Bar. He came right up to the bar where Mike worked, put his hand on the bar but did not sit down.

"Hello, Mike. I heard about your hotel. Nice place you've got here."

"You've got some nerve showing your face in here, Sam."

"Can I have a beer?"

"Like I said, you've got some nerve showing your face in here."

"Let me tell you my story, Mike. Let me have a beer, and after you hear my story, you can throw me out if you want to."

"Okay," Mike said, as he pulled a pint and placed in front of Sam. "But whatever you're selling, I ain't buying, and neither is anybody else in my place."

Sam pulled up a barstool and sat on it, took a pull on his cold beer.

"So what's your story?"

"It started in Bangkok, a year ago. I was down and out. I'd finally hit the end of the line, ran out of money, didn't have anyone or anywhere to turn to."

"That was bound to happen to you sooner or later Sam. You burnt so many bridges."

"Yeah, I know. I was hanging in there for a while. The last thing that worked for me was turning a profit off selling those old used flip phones."

"Flip phones?"

"Yeah, you know, those old Nokia things we used back in the nineties."

"Who the hell wants those things?"

"There's a market for them amongst the organized crime types. The Triads – the Chinese mafia – and the Thai mafia. They can't be tracked or triangulated, apparently."

"Ah, figures. Good business?"

"Yeah, but it was getting harder and harder to get my hands on what was already an extremely limited commodity, and the profit margin wasn't covering my costs in between. Then some outfit in Hong Kong started selling a line of brand new cheap rip-offs. They were manufacturing them after reverse-engineering the old technology, and that completely blew me out of the water in the used flip-phone business.

"I was totally at the end of my rope. So I put an ad out there on the internet. You know – Willing to do anything, anywhere, anytime, for any amount. Dirty deeds done dirt cheap. You know the deal."

"Sounds about your style. As far as I'm concerned, your name is Dirtbag in here. Always was, always will be."

"I suppose I deserve that," Sam said as he took another sip of beer. "Well anyway, I got a bite. A guy down in Singapore contacted me, told me to come down there, he had a job of work for me. No guns, nothing crazy. It sounded like a good deal, so I went.

"We met at his hotel, one of those great big new affairs, all glass and polished steel. Nobody hangs out in the lobby. My client was a Chinese gentleman. We shook hands, then he took me back to his room.

"There was an old military duffle bag on a side table. It had a lock on it. "Take this bag," he told me, "up to Vientiane." He handed me a piece of paper with an address on it. "You will go to this café, with the bag, and a man will come to you. You will know him because he will be wearing a black baseball hat. He will take you the rest of the way, and you will be paid at that time."

"I asked him how much for the job? It was a lot of money – twenty grand. So I said, I'm gonna need some dough up front. I need some operating funds, I'm kind of short. He said no problem, we'll pay you ten percent up front, the rest when you deliver the bag.

"Then I asked him, what's in the bag? It's not drugs, is it? I don't deal drugs."

"That's not the way I remember it," Mike said. "I seem to recall something about a bale of opium, up there in Ban Nong Seang."

"That was different. That was for the Hmong. They wouldn't soldier unless they got their pipe of opium every night. That was their thing. Besides, the opium was an Agency thing. I was seconded to them. An Air America bird brought the stuff in, I was just along for the ride. We landed Ban Nong Saeng, I kicked the bundle and we got the hell out of there. Who knows where the Company got their hands on the stuff."

"Sounds like an excuse to me."

"It's not an excuse, it's a reason."

"Go on with your story, Sam."

"He assured me there was nothing illegal in the bag. No drugs, no weapons. So I asked again, what's in it? When he opened the bag and showed me, my jaw dropped."

"What was it?"

"Buddha."

"A Buddha?"

"Yeah. But not any Buddha. I'd lifted this very same Buddha from a house in Bangkok, more than twenty years ago."

"What made this one so special?"

"I dunno, but trying to move it through the usual dealers and private collectors was insane. Everybody I showed that Buddha to got all excited. It was like the thing was radioactive, but nobody would tell me the story.

"As you know, the Thai people consider the Buddha statue to have a spirit, to be like a piece of the original Buddha himself. That's why there are laws about taking Buddhas outside of Thailand and selling them in antique stores and art galleries."

Mike nodded, and looked to the little altar over in the corner of the Long Bar. Every house and business establishment in Thailand had such a place to respect the Buddha, the spirits of the land, and the King.

"I didn't know the story on this Buddha, but apparently I'd gotten my hands on a real special Buddha. I had to move it fast, because the people I was showing it to were getting excited, and word was gonna get out on the street. In the end I practically gave it away."

"And now this Chinese guy was showing it to you again? The same Buddha?"

"The same Buddha. I was looking at it again, and I know it was the same. It was very distinctive. About eighteen inches tall, bronze with inlaid gold, and inset with jade. And OLD – it wasn't new. The thing looked a thousand years old. I've never seen a Buddha like it anywhere, before or since. Very unique."

"What was so special about it? Other than its obvious uniqueness, and its age?"

"I dunno, but handling that Buddha was the beginning of a twenty-year streak of bad luck for me."

"Bad karma?"

"Bad karma like you cannot believe. A twenty-year run where things went from bad to worse and ended in that run-down baht house hotel room in Bangkok."

"Yeah, well you've done enough shit, Sam, to gin up enough bad karma for ten lifetimes before any Buddha statue showed up."

"Yeah, I know, Mike," Sam said. He hung his head, humble.

"You know what your problem is, Sam? For the rest of us, it's a war. For you, it's one giant business opportunity and you don't give a damn what laws you break, whose toes you step on, or who catches splatter coming off the stunts you pull. You're an out of control frikkin' war criminal, dammit!"

Sam took a pull of his beer. "The story continues," he said.

"So I'm looking at the thing, the Buddha, that had kicked off my two decades of bad juu-juu. And this Chinese guy is offering me more than enough money to have a new shot at everything I've lost and all I owed, just to tote it up to Vientiane. He was looking at me with that look the Orientals give you; you know the look, where their eyes just go right through you.

"We both knew toting that thing through Thailand was not exactly kosher. It was a cultural treasure and the authorities would claim it belonged to the Thai people, the Thai nation. Stolen artifact. And of course it symbolized – to me – twenty years of bad luck. But I needed the money, so I said I'd do it.

"There were special instructions, he was very specific – I was to take the trains."

"Why the trains?"

"Couldn't risk moving this thing by air – couldn't have it showing up in the security x-ray machines, right? And I couldn't drive it up there, the Thai police are always running roadblocks on the outskirts of cities, especially at night. So it had to be the trains."

"So you had to haul this thing all the way up the Malay peninsula, up to Bangkok, then on up north to Nong Kai, and across the Mekhong to make your way to Vientiane?

"Yes, nowadays the train goes to the Friendship Bridge at Nong Kai, on the Thai side of the Mekong. The train crosses into Laos, to Thanaleng station just outside of Vientiane. The café where I was to be picked up was down a street, a dirt road actually, about a quarter mile from the station."

"How'd it go? Smooth sailing?"

"Oh my God."

"Bad, huh?"

"Worse. We sealed the deal, the Chinese businessman handed me two thousand up front, ten percent to cover my expenses, and I took the bag back to my hotel. Walking through the streets with the thing on my back, every step of the way I felt like I was going to be jumped, or some Singaporean cop was going to hold me up and ask what's in the bag.

"I needed to get a new bag, of course. I couldn't haul a military duffle bag all the way up the Malay peninsula, all the way through Thailand and across the Mekhong River into Laos. That's crossing three international borders. The duffle bag would attract attention going through customs, it had the smuggler look all over it.

"So I diverted through the little twisted alleyways down by Bugis Street to shop for a backpack. Something that wouldn't attract as much attention. Trying to make my way through those crowds with the duffle bag on my back wasn't easy, especially with one hand on my wallet against pickpockets. I found a used backpack. It was big enough and nondescript enough not to attract any attention.

"Once I got to the hotel, I stayed put, I didn't go out. Just me and the bag. I was staying in one of those cheap Southeast Asian hotels and I didn't trust the help not to go through my backpack. I ordered room service – not that I had much of an appetite.

"The whole time I was laying there in my hotel room, I couldn't get to sleep. It was like the backpack had this . . . presence . . . I couldn't sleep, I could barely take my eyes off the thing. It was like there was some kind of . . . mysterious force . . . emanating from the backpack.

"The next morning I was already exhausted before I even set off. Due to the vagaries and intricacies of state-to-state relations and negotiations, no train currently exists that can take you from Singapore to the heart of the Malaysian interior, let alone all the way to Bangkok. I hopped the Malaysian Railways shuttle train that runs between Woodlands Checkpoint and Johor Bahru Sentral, the closest Malaysian transport hub to Singapore. I could have taken a taxi, but the traffic jams on the Causeway are horrific. Taking the train is the only way to go.

"The kimchee started getting deep the minute I got off the metro train in Johor. I felt like everyone was looking at me, and then sweating it through customs and immigration over in Malaysia. The only thing I had going for me is nobody smuggles stuff from Singapore to anywhere except by sea. The customs officer simply looked at my passport, stamped it and handed it back, but my blood pressure was up, let me tell you.

"Doing the trains in Southeast Asia is a great way to travel, by the way. It's definitely the way to go, and under normal circumstances it would have been an enjoyable trip. The first-class carriages have these swivel chairs, almost like enormous barber chairs, and one can sit back with a beer in the little holder of the armrest and enjoy watching the palm trees and the rice paddies roll by, villages tucked into groves of banana trees and mango trees, green hills in the distance.

"Under normal circumstances, that is. My situation was anything but normal, of course.

"First of all, I was extremely worried about going to the toilet. I'd be leaving the bag behind, right? But sooner or later you have to go, it's inevitable. When you've got to go, you've got to go. Everybody else was getting up to go, and there wasn't any place to go if one did steal a bag. Anyway, there was a porter in the first class carriage. I purposely did not look anxiously at the bag as I got up to make my way to the end of the carriage. Didn't want to draw overt attention to the thing.

"When I got back, however, the first thing I did was look at the bag, before I could catch myself and not look. And damned if the thing didn't look like someone had moved it, perhaps opened it and gone through my things.

"Now I was stuck with a dilemma; do I take it down and check is the Buddha still there? To do so would attract everyone's attention to the bag, of course, and whatever might be within it. To not do so, well, if my precious cargo had been lifted, it would be essential to know before the train came to the next stop. Unless the thief tossed it off the train to a waiting accomplice, or perhaps jumped with it."

"Mind playing games with itself," Mike suggested.

"Yeah! In any case, I didn't have to check it. It sounds strange, but I had this feeling – I can't describe it – the Buddha was in the bag. I knew from just looking at it up there in the luggage rack. It was like the bag was pulsing as I looked at it."

"Pulsing?" Mike asked.

"Like it was almost breathing. There was a kind of energy pulsing out of that bag and I could feel it. I can't explain it, but it is what it is.

"I was getting paranoid, of course, and it was only to get worse with every passing minute and every mile of track.

"Train from Johor Bahru takes about four or five hours to Gemas, the railway junction between the Malaysian east and west coast rail networks. It had already been a long day by the time. Now I was doing the bag drag at Gemas Station, to get on the North-South Line that goes all the way to Thailand.

"From Gemas, the train stops at Kuala Lumpur." Sam went on. "I personally like KL," he said, using the expat's acronym for Kuala Lumpur. "It's like the beating heart of the country, rising out of the dense, mysterious rainforests. I had to stay overnight in Kuala Lumpur, which suited me fine. I prefer KL so many ways more than Singapore. Singapore is too manicured, too orderly for me. Beneath its modern skyscrapers, KL is still strangely messy and variegated.

"I stayed in a low-budget Chinese hotel near the station, had them bring a double order of satay to my room. I'd have preferred to hang out at a street café and have satay and beer while I watched the world go by, but I didn't want to take my eye off the bag with my precious cargo.

I couldn't hang out in the street and risk having the bag snatched away from me.

"The next morning I caught the morning train to Padang Besar, the Thai border crossing, about six hours up the track. The train stops at Ipoh, Butterworth, Langkawi, Alor Setar, Arau, all tourist destinations, and many other smaller stops along the way.

"The scenery's great, classic Southeast Asia; rice paddies and coconut palms, villages in the distance. And you can see the concrete bunkers, dotted all over the place where roadways cross the rice paddy dikes. Relics from the War, when the Japanese came down the Malay peninsula and overwhelmed the British forces.

"Right," Mike nodded. He'd seen the bunkers. It occurred to him that people still referred to World War II as "The War", despite the fact there'd been so many wars since then.

"Padang Besar is the rail crossing between Malaysia and Thailand, of course. In Malay it means 'big field'. The Thai town across the border has the same name, Haad Yai, although Malays refer to it as Pekan Siam, which means "Thai Town".

"At Padang Besar, everybody has to get off the train and go through the station to cross over into Thailand. This of course meant another encounter with customs officers. Hauling my bag through the open-air station in the tropic heat, I was sweating like a pig by the time I presented my passport. All I could hope was my somewhat respectable middle-aged demeanor and conservative haircut would preclude a search of the bag.

"Haad Yai is a quaint, relatively quiet southern Thai town, as you're probably aware. There was about an hour before the train to Bangkok departed. I had to stretch my legs, so I took a walk through the placid streets of the city. There isn't much in the way of adventure in Haad Yai, which suited me fine. To me, the city harks back to an older, simpler Malaysia or the old Singapore one sees more in postcards. Life functions at a more mundane, slower pace.

"No rush, of course. If I was in a hurry I'd have flown, but that was off the menu of course. Haad Yai to Bangkok takes about eighteen hours. I climbed into my berth on the sleeper car, then woke up nearly a day later in another city, another culture, another country, about a thousand kilometers north of my start point.

"Most people find riding the rails up from Malaysia relaxing. That's how it's always been for me. This trip was different. By the time the train pulled into Bangkok I was physically exhausted. Despite the urgency of my mission, I had to get off the train. My plan was to find a hotel room, rest and refresh and hopefully get some sleep before the final leg of the journey.

"It didn't work out this way, of course. I should have thought this thing out in advance. Bangkok is a bustling metropolis, something extraordinary and exciting is always happening, in all directions, in three dimensions, everywhere you look, everywhere you go. I should have gotten off the train in sleepy little Hua Hin and stayed overnight down there. Instead I was staggering through the fast paced, incredibly overcrowded streets of Bangkok with my precious cargo in my bag on my back, clutching at the shoulder straps with both hands hoping and praying I didn't fall prey to a bag-snatcher or a surreptitious taxi driver.

"I planned on splurging it a bit – I had a lot of cash burning a hole in my pocket, so I went for a higher-end hotel down in my old stomping grounds, the Sukhumvit district. There are all kinds of high-end hotels over there. I simply couldn't put up with a low-end flophouse. Not with my precious cargo.

"You know what happened, though – right?"

"What?"

"No credit card. I couldn't get a room anywhere along up and down Sukhumvit Road."

"Oh, yeah. I guess that's right."

"So I waved down a tuk-tuk and caught a ride down to Chinatown. I can't figure out how to get to Chinatown on the skytrain, and I didn't want to risk a taxi. At least with a tuk-tuk, if things start going sideways, it's easy to bail out.

"And so, I ended up back in a cheap Chinese hotel again, just like in Singapore. And again, I didn't want to walk around the streets with my precious cargo slung over my shoulder so I stayed in my room, had the staff bring me some food. At least I could get some sleep.

"Or at least, that's what I hoped, but any kind of deep, restful sleep eluded me. My dreams were haunted by images of the Buddha statue, floating around. It was like the statue itself was tormenting me. There was a deep, pulsing drumbeat, almost a heartbeat, but loud, overwhelming. I tossed and turned.

"The next morning when I looked at myself in the mirror, I looked dreadful. So much for getting some sleep. Staying the night in Bangkok in order to get some kind of rest had turned out to be a mistake. It was time to get down to Hua Lamphong Station and catch the Northeast Line train for the rest of my journey.

"It's an overnighter to Nong Kai. If you've ridden the trains in Thailand you know the deal. They pull into these little country town stations and the kids come on board, walk down the aisles selling their wares. Barbecued chicken which is absolutely delicious, splayed out on bamboo sticks, sticky rice with red beans in it, sold in the tubes of bamboo it was cooked in with a folded-up banana leaf for a stopper. And Thai ice tea, rich and sweet, in plastic bags held at the top with a rubber band with a straw sticking out. One things for sure, you'll never die of hunger or thirst on a Thai train.

"For the most part I stayed put, keeping an eye on my backpack. But again, the dilemma of having to go eventually emerged. I dealt with it again by waiting until we'd pulled out of a station, had picked up enough speed to where I felt it was generally safe enough to get up, leaving my bag in the overhead rack, and make my way to the W.C.

"I tried to get some sleep, sitting there in my swivel chair, but it was like the hotel room in Bangkok all over again. The bag above me seemed to have a presence. A sort of, I don't know, energy pulsated from it, a sort of gravitational beam or something focused directly into my conscience. Every clickety clack of the train over the rails was the pulsing heartbeat again, beating inside my head like a drum. I eventually passed out from sheer exhaustion, caught a couple hours badly needed sleep.

"I was up around dawn, had to make my way to the W.C. I still had trepidation about leaving the bag with my precious cargo up there in the luggage rack, but again there wasn't anything I could do about it, so I dealt with it.

"We were getting close to our destination. The train pulled into one of those northeastern cities, must've been Khon Kaen, and I had the usual for breakfast; sticky rice and barbecued chicken. I washed it down with a bottle Singha beer, I needed something to settle my nerves.

"The scenery we were passing through was no longer the lush green rice paddies and palm trees we passed through a few days back, on the peninsula. Everything was high and dry, with those steep jungled limestone karsts off in the distant horizon. And not so many water buffaloes these days, either. Farmers are all using those motorized 'rice rockets' to plow their fields, sort of like a lawn mower with large tractor tires."

"That's progress," Mike said. "Nowadays the buffalo are the basis of the Thai 'beef' industry."

"Yes. Well, we finally pulled into Nong Kai around noon. There's a break before the train crosses the Friendship Bridge into Laos. You have to get off the train to clear immigration on the Thai side, before the train crosses the Mekong into Laos. That's the way they do it, I don't know why.

"I was so close to my destination, so excited I had a hard time prying myself from my seat. I had to navigate my way through one last customs barrier with that Buddha in my bag.

"The interface with the customs officer was the usual sweat bath. After intensely studying my passport and eyeballing me up and down, the officer stamped my passport with an almost reluctant air. I guess I looked like one of those adventure travelers, with my unkempt appearance and my backpack. I took my passport and got back on the train.

"It was strange. As I sat there on the train clutching the bag on my lap, with the Buddha in it, my heart was going like a jackhammer. I should have been relaxed, or maybe tired from my journey, but instead I was experiencing an adrenalin rush like anything we ever did in combat. I guess I was just overcome with anticipation on what awaited me on the other side of the Mekong, looking forward to handing over the precious cargo and collecting my paycheck.

"Finally, the loudspeakers announced the train was leaving to cross over into Laos. People clambered back onboard, the whistle blew and the train shuddered as it began its forward movement. My heart was beating and my head was swimming, I felt like I was on drugs.

"Its less than a mile from the Nong Kai station across the bridge to the other side but it seemed to take ages. But when the train lurched to a halt at Thanaleng Railway Station, it somehow seemed anti-climactic. I was here, I'd arrived. Now all I had to do was find the tea shop, sit down and wait for my linkup and its payday. Or at least that's what I thought.

"I stumbled out into the street. My legs were still numb from sitting for so long, and from this strange dizziness, and the bright sunlight and the heat of the day intensified the sensation. The teashop was a ways down a dusty dirt road, not right across the street from the station like the Chinese guy in Singapore had said. All my fellow travelers were getting into air-conditioned minibuses for the six mile drive into Vientiane and here I was staggering down a dirt road in the noonday sun, like 'Mad Dogs and Englishmen'. Oh well, its Laos, after all. The place always was the boondocks.

"I found the tea shop – tea shack is more like it - sat down and ordered an ice tea. I looked around, wondering when my contact would show up. I was the only farang in the place, so he wasn't going to have a hard time identifying me.

"Sure enough, as soon as my tea was served I was joined by an Oriental gentleman in a black baseball cap. "I am Loh," he said simply. I introduced myself, and Loh got right down to brass tacks, unusual for an Oriental. He indicated the bag on the chair next to me, pointing with his chin. "This is it?"

"Yes," I said. "You want it here? Now?"

"No," he said. "Not here. Cannot show money, here this place." What he said made perfect sense. I was about to get the payday of a lifetime, in cash, and I sure as hell didn't want the whole neighborhood in this back end of beyond knowing about it. We left the teashop and got into Loh's pickup truck, one of those king cab Toyota HiLux things. I put the bag in the back seat, climbed into the passenger seat.

"I had no idea where we were going, I simply had to trust the man. What I'd imagined would be a ten or twenty minute ride turned into over an hour out into the countryside, away from Vientiane. I got a bit worried, but what could I do about it? I wondered if this was going to be a rip off, but then I kept telling myself that would make no sense. They trusted me with the Buddha all this way, now it was my turn to trust them.

"We arrived at a temple complex dwarfed by the enormous jungled karst mountains it was nestled into. Being at a holy place reassured me that things were going to be copacetic. Loh parked the truck, got out and I followed him across the temple compound, around the main temple building and out the back gate of the compound. There was a long stairway with dragons on either side, golden dragons. The stairway up the mountain was so steep and so high I couldn't make the top of it.

"We finally came to the top of the stairs. A path way with irregular stones set in it for paving led around the heavily jungled mountainside. Working gangs of monks were working on improving the pathway and cutting more steps into the cliff. The monks wore simple shifts of dark maroon, not the full saffron robes they normally wear; these were forest monks. They carried buckets of wet concrete on yokes over their shoulders or baskets of gravel and dirt on their heads. Their thin frames were covered with ropy muscles under skin bronzed a deep brown by the sun, their veins bulged out like drainage pipes. I marveled at their physical strength and endurance, on a vegetarian diet, no less. The monks paid scant attention to us as we made our way further upward.

"The jungle was everywhere now, and due to the altitude – I estimated us to be at least two thousand feet above sea level – it was cool and damp. The sun was going down by the time we arrived at a simple wooden hut. Loh indicated that I should remove my shoes, and we went inside.

"It was dark inside, the only light a few candles at a small alter on the far wall, with a few sticks of sandalwood incense smoldering. The floor was covered with tatami rice straw mats on the floor. We both sat on the floor, and I placed the bag between us.

"An older monk entered the dark room. That is, older than the working monks we had passed on the climb up here. Loh gave the traditional wai greeting, hands pressed together at forehead level, and bowed all the way to the floor. Because I know my manners, I did the same thing of course. The monk nodded as he sat down across from us, on a platform slightly higher where we sat on the tatamis. Then another monk entered the room, even older still. Loh kowtowed again, and so did I. He sat on a platform a level higher than the first monk. The first monk spoke but I could not understand what he said. I don't understand Lao or whatever dialect or language it was he was speaking.

"Open the bag," Loh whispered. "Show them the Buddha."

"I opened the bag and withdrew the Buddha with trembling hands. I held it out because I felt it should not be on a level lower than any person sitting in the room. The monks both gave a *wai* to the Buddha statue and so did Loh, and I mentally winced for not doing so myself before handling it. The first monk arose, took the Buddha from me and placed it on the alter. Several more monks entered the room and seated themselves on the platform with the first monk, and all began chanting.

"Buddhist chanting is very drone-like. It has a lot of focus and is very hypnotic. I don't know how long the chanting took place because any sensation of time was lost. It seemed like fifteen minutes, but I had the feeling that it went on for hours.

"The chanting finally came to an end. Loh informed me that they had put the blessing into the Buddha statue, to make its spirit happy in its new home. The older monk, the one seated on the highest platform, said something and two of the acolytes went to the alter, gave deep kowtows before the Buddha, then picked the statue up and brought it to him. Another acolyte placed a large brass platter before the older monk, who then did something quite curious.

"The older monk turned the Buddha sideways and began knocking on the lower portion of the statue, which was like a pedestal, or a dais of some sort. As he knocked, a wide plug loosened on the flat bottom of the statue. The monk removed the plug with some effort, and what looked like a combination of sand and ash and pieces of stone or possibly very old bone poured out onto the brass platter.

"The older monk then looked me in the eye and spoke in English, which surprised me."

"We wish to thank you, sir, for returning to us the relics of the Lord Buddha. This," he indicated the pile on the platter before him, "are ashes, fragments of bone and teeth of the Lord Buddha."

"I stared at what I thought was a pile of dirt and stones. It was almost unimaginable that this was the remains of the actual Buddha, who lived and walked this Earth over two thousand five hundred years ago.

"The older monk continued. "The Ashokavadana narrates how the great King Ashoka divided the relics of Lord Buddha into eighty-four portions and had stupas built over them throughout the regions he ruled. Many of the remains were taken to other countries. This is the portion of the relics that were given to our country, our people, two thousand years ago. These relics have been missing, stolen from this temple many years ago when the Communists took control of our country."

"Woah . . ." Mike whispered.

"Yes, I was thrown for a loop, I can tell you."

"So the whole thing was about the dirt? I mean the ashes?"

"Always was, apparently. The Buddha statue itself was just a container for the relics. The dirt, as you put it."

"That's pretty heavy."

"Yes," Sam said. "Ironic, eh?"

"How so?"

"Here I am, the Dirt Bag, transporting a bag of dirt, a dirt bag . . . albeit, very special dirt."

"What happened next?"

"More chanting. The older monk explained were thanking me, blessing me with a very special blessing. It was just like the first round of chanting, the same hypnotic effect and the strange sensation regarding the passage of time. I really don't know how long it went on.

"I'm not Buddhist, I'm not really very religious at all, but when it was over, I sensed a definite vibe. A sort of magnetic field all around my body is the only way I can describe it.

"When Loh and I emerged from the little hut it was sunup. We'd been in there all night. It had been a full day the day before but somehow, I didn't feel tired, I didn't feel anything like the way I'd felt the day before, getting off the train. Coming down the mountain, I felt like I was walking on clouds. I felt like I'd gotten my batteries recharged."

"Maybe that's exactly what happened," Mike suggested.

"Yes, well, that's certainly one way of looking at it," Sam acknowledged, downing his glass of beer.

"Want another one?" Mike asked. Sam was right, his story was worth a beer or three.

"Yes, thanks," Sam said. "There's more to the story, though. I'm not done yet."

"What, the money?"

"Well, yeah. I got paid. Loh took me to his place and handed me a bag full of cash. US dollars. Twenties, fifty banded stacks of them. I handed him two stacks back. "You overpaid me, Loh, there was an advance." He told me to keep it, as a bonus for getting the job done right, and on time."

"Nice touch" Mike said. "Something you don't see very often in our line of work."

"No, you don't. Anyway, I made my way back to the station, took the train back across to Thailand, and of course this time I had as much if not more to sweat about, crossing the border."

"What do you mean?"

"The cash, man. Transporting more than ten thou over an international border, you know. Just as illegal as smuggling a gold Buddha, maybe more so."

"I take it you had no problems."

"None, and I wasn't nervous or sweating like when I was bringing the Buddha up from Singapore. Like I said, I was walking on clouds, and I felt like I had a golden aura around my body."

"Hmmm."

"Yeah! The customs officials just smiled and stamped my passport like I was a member of the family. No poker face routine, nothing."

"Those monks up on the mountain must have slapped some pretty strong juu-juu on you."

"It gets weirder."

"Okay." Mike served Sam his beer. "Here you go. Go on with the story."

"Well, I was kicking around Nakhon Ratchisima – you know, Khorat – to relax a bit before hitting Bangkok again. I decided to go to the casino, to bank my money. Easier than toting all that cash around everywhere I went, and I could bypass the banking laws. Of course, as long as I was in the casino and I was in such a good mood, I decided to play a bit of cards."

"A good night at the tables?"

"Unbelievable."

"How unbelievable?"

"I doubled my money."

"Woah, that IS unbelievable."

"Just wait, it gets even crazier. Walking out of the casino, I bought a lottery ticket . . ."

"Oh, you've got to be joking!"

"No, I bought a lottery ticket and gave it to one of the girls sitting around in front of the coffee shop next door to the casino. The girl had been sidling up to me, trying to make sweet on me, and it was my way of getting her to go away."

"Oh, OK."

"I mean, who ever heard of a farang playing the lottery in Thailand, right?"

"Right."

"The next day I went down to the casino and the girl and all her friends were jumping up and down and going totally nuts!"

"Huh?"

"That ticket had been the winning number!"

"Do I sense a sort of pattern playing out here?"

"I'm telling you, I was beginning to wonder. So that night when I went back into the casino, I kept my bets kind of low. I'd already attracted too much attention to myself, I didn't want to break the bank and have them run me out of town on a rail or anything. Even still . . ."

"You kept winning?"

"Couldn't lose a hand if my life depended on it."

"Some kind of Midas Touch?"

"Something's going on. Anyway, it was time to collect my winnings and get the hell out of town.

"I didn't hang out in Bangkok very long – that is not the place for me these days. It's too fast paced, too much going on, and too many eyes in too many places looking me up and down. Either street hustlers trying to rip me off, or cops or some kind of international law enforcement, all trying to rip me off."

"So you show up here."

"Yeah, I really need a place to cool my heels. But before I caught the train out of Bangkok at Hua Lamphong Station, I did one last thing."

"Let me guess," Mike said, almost sarcastically.

"Yep. I bought a lottery ticket." Sam produced the ticket, placed it on the bar. "Tell you what, Mike. If you put me up here in your hotel, I can pay six months in advance, in cash." Sam lifted the bag and placed it on the barstool next to him, tapping it to indicate its contents. "Or you can have the lottery ticket. Choice is yours."

Mike took the ticket, looked at it. It had Thai lettering but he could read the numbers. A winning lottery ticket would be worth twice of what Sam would pay for a room. IF this was a winning lottery ticket. "Same ol' Sam the Scam Artist, eh?" he laughed.

"Hey, I've got the cash if you'd rather go that way," Sam shrugged. "Just thought I'd make the offer. Don't blame you if you prefer cash."

Mike sized up his customer. "I tell you what, Sam. Your story rings true, even though the saying goes 'believe nothing what you hear and only half of what you see.' There's something about a game of chance. I'll take the ticket. You're up in cabana 504. I'll see the cashier, Leena Wan, in the morning and tell her about the pay arrangements."

"Thanks, Mike, old buddy."

Mike winced at this, coming from an old nemesis.

"You won't regret it."

"Ha! We'll see." Mike placed the lottery ticket up on the wall, behind a very old, very expensive bottle of single malt Scotch, and went to tend to the other customers.

The next morning Mike went to the bar, retrieved the lottery ticket and took it down to cashier's office. "Here you go, Leena Wan. Let me know if this number's any good."

Leena Wan took the ticket, looked at it, and clicked over to the Thai National Lottery website. She looked at the ticket again, then back at the screen, then at the ticket again. Then she sat back in her chair, eyes still glued to the screen. The ticket shook in her trembling hands. Leena Wan could barely whisper,

"Oh, mistah Mi'e . . . mistah Mi'e . . ."

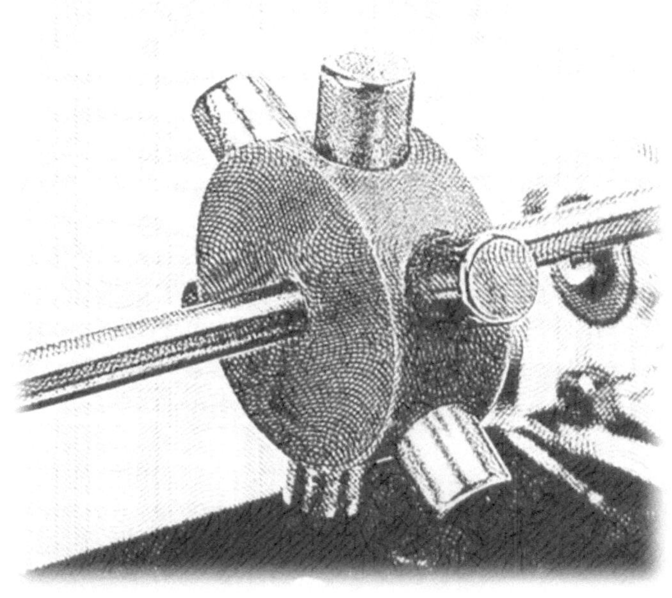

Chapter 10

The Machine

"It started with a phone call . . ."

Mike sensed a good story coming on. "Go on," he said, as he served a beer.

The speaker – Sean - was a man of medium height and build, a bit on the muscular side like a rugby player, with the scars and the broken nose to go with it.

"This guy - well known successful businessman - called me, told me he'd been looking at my profile on LinkedIn for some time now, was impressed by my resume, my writings, comments on posts, that I'm articulate, etc. So, I'm wondering where this is going. "Uh huh," I grunt, and he gets right down to the point:

"I've invented a perpetual motion machine," he told me. "We call it 'The Machine'..."

"Right away I realize that I'm talking with a madman, of course, and looking back, I almost wish I'd hung up right then and there. But like a fool I didn't. Curiosity got the better of me, and so I stayed on the line.

"OK," I said, "This is a physical impossibility, of course, against the laws of physics, but don't let me stop you. Please continue..."

"Yes," said Mike, "I'm dying to hear this." The concept of a perpetual motion machine was intriguing, and he understood Sean's curiosity driving him to stay on the phone.

Sean continued. "Ha, I understand where you're coming from," the businessman told me, "but bear with me for a minute. Stop and think for a minute Sean, what such a machine - if it could actually be - would be capable of doing?"

"Well," I said, "only one thing comes to mind. If such a machine were possible - that's a big if - I suppose you could use it to produce power."

"That is in fact exactly what we have done" he said. "Now think of the possibilities of THAT."

"Well, you'd put the fossil fuel and nuclear power generation industries out of business, and give solar and wind industries a run for their money."

"This thing is huge, Sean, and it's getting ready to explode all over the country. We already have investors; Bill Gate's people, and Warren Buffet, to name a few. They've fronted up one hundred million of seed money, and are ready to invest five billion once we've got the production lines rolling."

"OK," I said, "So how can I help you?"

"Well, as you know, I've put together a pretty big association of Special Operations types over the years, through my social media presence - Peace Professionals - and your name keeps coming up to the top of the list."

"As you can imagine, we're going to require a very significant security operation, around our manufacturing and installation, and then later around the installed machines themselves. A really big operation, and it's going to require a really imaginative security professional to run it - a guy like you. You've got a well-rounded background, an engineering degree, and experience in the power industry and the oil industry. But let me tell you a bit about our business model first."

"We're not here to put anybody out of business - we intend to supplement the existing power industry. As you know, the power generation capacity in North America - and everywhere else for that matter - is stretched thin as it is, and the power distribution grid is vulnerable to sabotage, if some bad actors - say, Iran or the North Koreans or whoever - wanted to really put the hurt on us."

"Right," I said, but I don't think he heard me. He was talking almost a mile a minute, and my mind was racing about a hundred miles an hour . . ."

"So what we're looking to do is set these things up at factories, all kinds of industrial facilities as standby or even primary power generators, large buildings, public transportation systems, everywhere, you name it."

"We will not sell any of the machines - they remain our property - and we're not trying to put anybody out of business. Quite the opposite. Can you imagine the implications if, overnight, all commercial enterprises in the developed world were suddenly freed up of 95% of their electric bills? And household residents as well. Suddenly the entire world has a lot more disposable income on hand."

"Right," I said. I was tracking on all of this.

"We can make them small or large. Anything from residential requirements, to the power requirements for a hospital, or a factory, or a large skyscraper. We can even hook them up in tandem to produce hundreds of megawatts - enough to power a large city."

"When it was finally my turn, I said, "Well, before I commit to anything, I'm going to have to have a look at this machine."

"Yes, of course. I'm going to send you a link to our site, and another link to a rolling password token. It's a twenty-digit password, randomly turning over so it's never the same."

I'm familiar with this kind of encryption, actually. It's been around for at least ten or fifteen years.

So I went to the site, looked at what they had. The machine was a large cylinder, about a meter tall and a meter in diameter, sitting in a large black plastic tub, with an axle or an armature sticking out the top of it, with something on the end of it spinning like a wind vane.

The whole cylinder was wrapped in silver-colored insulation. They had it hooked up to a digital multimeter, which gave power readouts, and a bank of really bright lights. The claim was that this thing was actually generating power.

Afterwards, Al - the businessman - called me back. "Well, what do you think?"

"Well," I said, "I'm not sure I know what I was looking at, and I know a thing or two about power generation. I'd like to look at it in person, actually have an opportunity to walk around the thing."

"Yes, sure."

"A date was set up and they flew me out to New Mexico, where they had a larger industrial sized module set up at Los Alamos - the Federal test site facility. It took me the better part of two hours to get clearance at the gate, then they led me into this large building and right there in the middle of the room was The Machine.

"It did what they said it did. I walked around it, and unless there was a power feed coming up from beneath the floor, this thing was producing power, and there was almost no heat being generating off it, either.

"What I was witnessing was against the laws of physics, of course, and those laws - unlike our written laws, that police enforce - simply cannot be broken.

"The only way The Machine could possibly work was by somehow harnessing some kind of energy waves. Tesla had suggested this, back in the twenties. This was the only way I could figure the thing worked.

"I signed on to the team. I negotiated a hefty remuneration, of course, firstly because I'm worth it, and secondly because the scope of the project was going to be enormous.

"They were basically asking me to physically secure their devices, their entire manufacturing facilities and corporate footprint, and on top of that somehow keep the Chinese or whatever bad actors out there from getting their hands on one of these things so they couldn't take it apart and reverse engineer it.

"As it turned out, the threat - when it emerged - came from a vector I never would have suspected, completely blindsided me.

"My own people . . .

"Almost overnight every disgruntled Green Beret, Recon Marine, Navy SEAL - you name it - was out there trying to sabotage the machines.

"As far as I could determine, it was the security forces from the nuclear power industry trying to shut us down - we represented the end of a paycheck for them, and they weren't going down without a fight.

"Them, and the out-of-work workers of the oil industry, who mistakenly blamed The Machine for their situation.

"You heard about that sniper attack that shut down the electrical grid in San Jose a few years ago? That was the first hit.

"How did you deal with them?" Mike asked.

"How DO you deal with an existential threat like that? I could only put so much physical security on the devices themselves, and unless a barrier is covered by some kind of reactive armed security, there's always a way around it.

"So what happened?"

"Ultimately, we had to start stacking the devices within heavily protected perimeters, with intrusion detection systems, armed security officers, etcetera."

"Was that enough to stop them?"

"Well, yes, but this was wreaking havoc on the business model. Suddenly, what was supposed to be down to almost zero per megawatt hour was approaching - and in some cases exceeding - cost per megawatt hour for conventionally generated electrical power!

"There was no way of stopping them. The rat bastards - my former colleagues - had taken it to themselves to make war against The Machine, as it were. All I could do was mitigate it where I could, and meanwhile watch a game-changing technology get shut down by modern day Luddites.

"The best paycheck I ever had was slowly withering on the vine.

"Surely there must have been something that could be done?"

"Nope. They – the saboteurs - successfully shut the thing down. The whole operation. It was the damnedest thing.

Here we had the solution to the world's energy challenges right in the palm of our hand, the capability to expand prosperity above and beyond anybody's wildest imagination, and the whole thing was being shut down by a bunch of mouth breathers doing drive-by's, slinging lead from the windows of their trucks."

"That's it?" Mike inquired. "They just gave up on a world changing idea without a fight?"

"What could they do? Sure, they made money, and there were still a few applications where The Machine could come in handy, but what factory or hospital or any other commercial operation wants to invest in something that is essentially a bullet magnet? There's enough concern out there about all these active shooter incidents as it is. Why buy into something that's going to guarantee a rifle being aimed in your direction?

"The final Kiss of Death was when the insurance agencies wrote in clauses jacking up their premiums to any property housing one of The Machines.

"My business patron - the mysterious guy who got me into this thing in the first place - called a meeting at the corporate HQ. Downtown Chicago, on the thirty second floor of The Machine building . . . The hairs were going up on the back of my neck as I walked from the elevator down the hallway to the big boardroom. If ever I felt I was walking into an ambush, this was it . . ."

"What did he have to say?"

"When I entered the room I suddenly know how General Custer felt at Little Bighorn . . . they were all there - the CEO, the COO, all the senior vice-presidents, all lined up behind that huge boardroom table, as big as an aircraft carrier.

"They basically accused me of being behind the shootings, doing it to create a threat that didn't exist, so as to create job security for myself. This was bullshit of course, but how do you disprove a negative?"

"What did you do?" Mike asked.

"What could I do?" Sean replied. "I denied it of course, but what good did that do? They'd made up their minds and that was that."

"So what happened??"

"I stood there and considered the implications of what was unfolding right before me. This meant my reputation was in ruins, of course, and in the security business a bad reputation means you're run out of the business on a rail."

"Surely you couldn't let anyone do that to you?"

"Well, I never go anywhere without a little insurance policy working for me. When I was in the Army, the radio to that big Spectre gunship orbiting overhead represented my insurance. In this case, it was a bit of technology but not quite as spectacular as "Spooky".

"I guess I have to inform you that this entire conversation has been recorded," I said, placing my smartphone down on the boardroom table. The corporate suits all looked at that thing like it was a pit viper, all coiled up and ready to strike."

"That cell phone is company property," the COO told me, with a smug look on his face. "You'll have to turn that over. Now, in fact."

"He looked like a toad as he said this, which was appropriate because as far as I was concerned he was a toad. Him and all the rest of the corporate suits staring me down.

"I shrugged, as if to say 'I guess you got me'. Now all the toads were looking smug, feeling all cocksure of themselves, they'd outsmarted the security guru. Well, maybe so and maybe not. They got their smartphone but none of them paid any attention to the expensive pen clipped in the upper left pocket of my suit jacket. The pen that was actually a recording device; audio and video.

"I walked out of that boardroom and the rat bastards had the uniformed security personnel waiting outside to escort me out of the building. Nice touch, I thought, wouldn't want to lose my pen on the way down to the lobby and out in the street.

"My next move was to get in touch with a lawyer I know. A girl I went to school with actually; her name is Martha. I told her everything that had happened.

"Illinois is an at-will employment state," Martha explained. "Employers can terminate an employee for any reason at all except an illegal reason. In other words, they could fire me for any reason or no reason at all."

"Yes, I understand this," I said. "But check out where they screwed up: when they bad mouthed me, made all those wild accusations just before they fired me, there was one individual in the room who wasn't a member of the company. The inventor of The Machine.

"The inventor wasn't a member of the company because all he wanted was the royalties on his patent. He wasn't even a stockholder - the royalties were worth far more than any shares of stock. So in other words, the CEO and the COO and all the senior vice presidents had slung their baseless accusations at me, slandered my character and given that as reason for letting me go – in front of a member of the public.”

Martha practically drooled when I showed her what I had on them. And I had it all recorded, legally. Audio and video. "Oh my God Sean, this is GOLD."

There was the whole anti-defamation thing, and the common law action of retaliatory discharge, which is one exception to the employee-at-will doctrine.

“We took them to court for everything they had. We won, and when I say we won, we won lock, stock and everything. I ended up with the whole company, which was sort of like winning the booby prize when you think about it, because now I had a business to run. Worse still, the business model was dead in the water and nobody wanted to touch this thing with a ten-foot barge pole.

“So what did you do?” Mike asked.

“I sold it,” Sean shrugged.

“To who? I thought you said the business model was dead?”

“Yes it was, but the item itself still had great value – to the right people. Do you know the story of the Iridium satellite phone?”

“Not really.”

"It came out in the late nineties – a satellite phone, as small as a cellphone, which could be used to make a call from anywhere in the world. A constellation of unique, single-user satellites served the Iridium phone. No need for towers or cell networks.

"Trouble was, the damn thing was so expensive, and the need was not there. At least not enough to drive a market for the thing. The company was on the verge of bankruptcy, when the US government stepped in. They saw the value in the phone and its satellites, and so they bought it. The Department of Defense bought the whole company for pennies on the dollar."

"So you sold your company to the US government?"

"Yes. Certain agencies saw the value of the Machine, and they had the money to meet my price. I'm not saying which agencies but their initials are C-I-A and N-S-A."

"Wow."

"Exactamundo. Wow. I'm suddenly rich overnight, beyond anyone's wildest dreams."

"What do you do now?"

"That's the problem – what DOES one do after an endeavor like THAT?" Sean lifted his beer to his lips. "Looking for the next thing, I suppose," he shrugged.

Outside in the inky darkness, way down at the base of the cliff, the surf boomed. The eternal, infinite drumbeat that preceded mankind and would continue long after mankind eventually found a way to extinguish itself. Sean looked out into the darkness and repeated, speaking as if to himself as much as to anyone listening.

". . . what DOES one do after an endeavor like THAT?"

Chapter 11

Down South

San Cristobal, capital of the Republic of El Cristobal, lies at the foot of Xiuhtecuhtli, the Mayan name of the volcano that looms ominously over the sleepy city. The ancient Mayans worshiped Xiuhtecuhtli, offered it human sacrifices – virgins were thrown in there annually. The soil on the slopes of Xiuhtecuhtli was particularly fertile for the cultivation of corn, manioc, cacao, potatoes and coffee. And for the Mayan's offerings and adoration, Xiuhtecuhtli would periodically reward them with eruptions that wiped their fields and villages away, and caused widespread havoc. And then the cycle would repeat and the Mayans would start over again.

San Cristobal is a throwback to a better time, a time before the hustle and bustle of modern life and all the complications that come with it overtook once pastoral Central American backwaters. The Economic Officer at the American Embassy suggested to me it's the success of agrarian programs. "There's more money in the countryside, the volcanic soil is incredibly fertile," he indicated the volcano through his office window. "Why go to the city? For a *campesino* to leave the farm and move to the city is to be sentenced to a life of poverty, a permanent slot on the lowest class of society."

And so San Cristobal remains a unique destination, a quiet provincial town, almost a time portal to the Good Old Days. Somehow I didn't take the concertina wire and the sandbagged fighting positions on all the official buildings seriously.

Meanwhile Xiuhtecuhtli smolders. The sacred mountain is a forgotten god, a looming presence, overlooking the activities of the mere mortals below . . .

* * *

This story begins with me getting my ass chewed:

"You had one job to do, Linnane. Get your team down to this dinky little place nobody has ever heard of - Cristobal - and ride herd on them while they do what they it is they do. One job! So how the hell did you end up in the middle of a revolution and overthrow the government . . . on YOUR FIRST NIGHT IN TOWN???"

"Well, Chief, it really all started back here in the States, at the airport, when I met my future self - or at least one of my future selves - getting on the airplane . . ."

"Huh?" Chief stared at me in consternation, and damn near bit through the butt of the half-smoked cigar that hung eternally from his lip.

*   *   *

We are all ghosts, haunting our past selves as we look back at them in our memories. There is the sensation of someone 'walking on our grave'. It comes with a shudder, and the hairs stand up on the back of your neck.

Time and space are not a linear progression of course – Einstein explains this to us. There are intersections and it is inevitable that people cross over; possible evidence of time travel or forms of 'immortality' are not unheard of. And so it was the day I encountered my future self, as I boarded my flight to the Republic of Cristobal.

Making my way down the aisle I noticed a tattoo on a gentleman's right arm; a Chinese dragon. The same Chinese dragon I have on my right arm. I mean, EXACTLY the SAME tattoo as mine . . .

Glancing over the gentleman I noticed he was tanned, dark hair without a trace of gray - this despite the fact he was evidently several years older than me, and dark piercing eyes. For all the life of me it seemed I was looking straight at an older version of myself. I was tempted to get his attention, roll up my sleeve and reveal my dragon.

Then I noticed something else. The gentleman – if indeed he was my future self, somehow physically present in this plane – was missing his left arm, directly above the elbow . . .

*   *   *

The night I checked into my hotel there was some kind of gathering outside in the street. It was a big crowd, with a woman leading the crowd, giving some kind of speech on a megaphone. Well I had reason to go outside. I wanted a bottle of wine, so I was making my way down the street to a local *tienda de vinos*. Coming back with my bottle of wine under my arm, I made it less than a block when it became evident the sidewalks were non-navigable, and so was the street, with all the people.

Somebody bumped me sideways and then I was in the middle of the crowd. The crowd was getting ugly, people were yelling at me in Spanish and I couldn't understand a word they were saying and things were on the verge of going out of control. When people started putting their hands on me I realized I had to do something to turn the sentiments of the crowd in my favor so I did the only thing I could think of - I hollered out at the top of my lungs:

"¡VIVA LA REVOLUCION!"

Those were the magic words, apparently, because right away everyone started yelling: *"¡VIVA! ¡VIVA!"* They picked me up and then I was crowd surfing as the mob made their way to this huge imposing building which I presumed was the Presidential Palace. All the while, you gotta understand, all I was doing was trying to stay alive.

There was a momentary lull at the bottom of the stairs leading up to the imposing edifice, so to keep the spirit of the thing alive I did the only thing that seemed natural at the time: I hurled my bottle of *vino rojo*. It shattered at the entrance of the marble wedding cake of a building, the crowd surged forward and the Presidential Honor Guard dropped their rifles and ran for their lives.

I guess you could say I christened the beginning of a new era . . .

* * *

The human wave that was the popular revolution busted down the doors of the Presidential Palace and poured in like a flood, dragging me along. Everywhere you looked they were ransacking the place, until we reached the offices of El Presidente himself; the Inner Sanctum of Power of the Republic. An uncomfortable quiet fell over the crowd, and one by one the rioteers dispersed until it was only the leaders of the mob - and myself - who remained. There was no sign of the former occupant of these ornate offices.

My comrades in arms looked about in wonder as it all sunk in, what they had just accomplished. Incredibly, they'd overthrown the hated dictator . . . with my help, apparently. Then the woman who had led the chanting with the megaphone - not one hour before - looked to me, excited. "Señor, now YOU are the new *EL PRESIDENTE ! ! !*" All her colleagues beamed, their smiling faces showing their approval at this logical conclusion.

El Presidente . . . the title had a nice ring to it. I felt a momentary surge of power go straight to my head.

Meanwhile the smoke had not yet cleared out in the palace grounds, they were still manning the barricades in the streets. In the palace courtyard my predecessor was being given the customary retirement ceremony for dictators who fail to make the last flight out of the city to the South of France . . . complete with blindfold and last cigarette . . . and it occurred to me that I'd just won the booby prize . . .

"Er, I think a better idea is for the Republic to have its first WOMAN *'La Presidente'* - think of the legitimacy in the eyes of the international community - much more beneficial for leveraging grants and loans from the World Bank and the international community, no? - versus a gringo like me who can only order a beer in Spanish. I think I can serve the Republic better in a more utilitarian role . . . Minister of Agriculture, perhaps?

Agriculture means farmland, and as far as I was concerned, the further away I could get from all the madness going on in the capital city, the better. As soon as possible I caught the train to the interior, way up in the mountains, to inspect the state of agriculture in Republica de San Cristobal.

There was much to see in the countryside. An afternoon was spent exploring an ancient Mayan pyramid. It was fascinating to clamber about its step sides, to climb the steep staircase up its center. I imagined the priests and acolytes conducting the Ceremony of the Sun. Did they actually perform human sacrifice, and were these volcanic stones once drenched in blood and gore?

Meanwhile the thing about the arm had been bothering me; the premonition was weighing on my mind. I was really anxious about the possibility of losing my arm. It was a tricky thing. What does one do when one has had such a vivid premonition? Such a significant indicator of a future mishap?

We finally arrived at our first destination and *los campesinos* were waiting, their bright smiling faces beaming as they presented their harvest. Unbelievable. Simply unbelievable. I was looking at more cannabis than I'd ever seen in my life! Marijuana, Mary Jane, hemp, reefer, dope, more weed than I could ever imagine existed even, dried and cured, bales and bales of the stuff. I mean, there was a LOT of grass! Enough to stone an army . . .

"But where are the food crops?" I asked, incredulous.

"Bah!" they snorted and hissed. "Thees ees better *Señor!* Thee ees *mucho dinero!*" And of course they were right. Any poor bastard can slave away growing corn and beans – this was a cash crop. But how could I apply for grants from the World Bank? "And there ees MORE, *Señor!*" they exclaimed as they walked me over to the poppy fields and the coca plants growing on the mountainside.

Of course I took notice of the scowling *hombres* with the military-style caps and crossed bandoliers, toting assault rifles and shotguns. As of any drug-producing operation, this was far from any sort of pastoral idyll.

I put my face in my hands and shook my head; no, no, no a thousand times no, this was not happening to me. Somehow I'd gone from a trip to the bottle shop to the de facto leader of a street revolution to candidate for *El Presidente* to the head representative and ministerial administrator of a national level drug growing operation. How the hell was I going to get out of this mess?

My senior staff assistant sensed my stress and anxiety. "What you need *Señor,* where you must go, are *los aguas termales minerales* – the mineral hot springs."

This didn't sound like a half bad idea. Anything to get me away from the drug fields and those heavy rifle-toting characters.

We made our way towards the mineral hot springs, first by truck until the trails became almost impassable. We then took an ox cart up the slopes of Xiuhtecuhtli, the smoldering volcano which presided over the entire countryside like a sulking god. A guide accompanied us, one of the *campesinos*, who prattled on in a dialect that I assumed was a mix of Spanish and Mayan.

My assistant translated; "This flowering tree is a powerful hallucinogen, if you take this flower you will go directly to the mental hospital. But the flower is very good; if you place the flower beneath your pillow you will sleep soundly, the deepest most restful sleep.

"This plant is inedible, it is poisonous. If you take the seeds and eat them, you will transform into a crazy animal and you endanger yourself. One time, a *campesino* took the seeds and the next day they found him naked, trying to outrun a diesel locomotive.

"This little animal," our guide picked up a tiny snail, its shell smaller than the small buttons on a button-down collar shirt, with a curious purple stripe that followed the spiral pattern around its yellow shell, and held his finger out allowing it to travel to my hand. "This little animal can enter the body." At least that's what I thought I heard the translator say – he was speaking Spanish, after all, which I barely speak. I imagined he meant the premature form of the snail? Entering the body through the mouth, or the ear perhaps? I hated to think he meant the urethra, or the other orifice. "It enters the body and it will live inside the mind." He must have meant the brain but he used the word *mente* which means the mind, the consciousness. I shuddered at the thought of a snail occupying my consciousness. I place my finger to the hallucinogenic tree and observed the little fellow making its way across.

And then we arrived at the hot mineral springs, a primitive spa featuring bamboo huts and many pools constructed of haphazardly placed stones and mortar. The jungle canopy provided shade, and the steam of the hot springs rose up. It was impossible to see the entire area as it wound around the mountain. The springs were quite hot, but there were also pools for cooling off. Our guide took us up the mountain to the beginning of the springs, where a large placard announced:

"LAS AGUAS RICAS EN AZUFIRE"

(The Sulphur-Rich Waters)

"Embellacen la piel, el cabello y las uñas y mejoran la circulación sanguínea. Sus efectos analgésicos ayudan a disminuir grandamente el estrés y los Dolores musculares y artricos ya que mediante el proceso de osmosis el azufre y le resto de minerales medicinales son absobidors por las células del cuerpo . . ."

It went on:

". . . logrando asi beneficiarnos con sus propiedades antiinflamatorias, inmunoestimulantes y regeneradoras las cuales están científicamente

comprobadas desde hace más de 2000 años."
javascript:void(0)

As I continued to read the unusual Spanish verbiage I strangely began to completely understand every word:

"Embellishes the skin, the hair and the nails and aids the circulation of the blood. Its analgesic and anti-inflammatory effects greatly help decrease stress and muscular sickness and arthritis because through the process of osmosis, sulfur and the rest of the medicinal minerals are absorbed through the skin into the body cells thus achieving benefit with its anti-inflammatory, immuno-stimulants and regenerative properties which are scientifically proven over 2000 years."

We entered the waters and it was indeed very restful and relaxing, but the heat eventually drove us to the cooler pools. Then we'd return to the hot sulphur to soak some more and enjoy its rejuvenative effects which were quite noticeable.

My intent was to remain in the countryside for a week or more, as long as it would take to do a complete tour and determine the needs and capabilities of the plantations. By now my Spanish was perfect, which was odd because all I'd studied in school was French and Latin but there you have it. Odd because I was picking up more than just vocabulary and grammar, I was getting the slang and the local idioms and I even understood the Mayan dialect of the *campesinos*. There was something more; vivid dreams that seemed to follow into the waking state.

Visions of strange creatures from the bas-relief carvings around the pyramids, come alive and talking to me, advising me in my affairs in the countryside.

The volcanic rumblings and tremors were increasing in tempo, to almost daily, and yet the seismic instruments of the meteorological station located halfway up the volcano gave no indications in the signals they transmitted. The fantastic creatures that now spoke to me constantly – an enormous rooster-like bird, a surreal jaguar, a dog-headed man, an enormous feathered serpent – insisted it was necessary we climb the volcano. Our ascent of Xiuhtecuhtli, the ancient Mayan god, took over six hours, and every inch of the way I was totally out of my skull. I knew they were hallucinations, but they were absolutely real. As real as this bar we're standing in now, as real as the people around us even now as I speak.

When we got to the instrument station the problem with the transmissions was immediately obvious. A large volcanic boulder lay squat on top of what remained of the station – angle irons and wires and the steel instrument housing protruded out like a large insect squashed beneath a giant's toe. There was a rumbling, quite a shaker, and Xiuhtecuhtli coughed a large red hot missile that landed like a mortar round less than half a football field away. Xiuhtecuhtli coughed again and this time a cloud of volcanic ash spilled over the crater and rolled towards us. We ran for our lives, of course.

Xiuhtecuhtli was in eruption.

The evacuation was chaos. The railway was an early casualty of the volcanic ash and the red hot, semi-molten boulders Xiuhtecuhtli was spitting out. The dirt roads and trails out of the hinterland were jammed with ox carts and donkey carts and ancient trucks overloaded until their suspension groaned and hundreds of thousands of *campesinos* on foot, some pushing bicycles laden with possessions, some beating hapless horses and donkeys.

It took us the better part of two weeks to make our way out of the disaster area. At night we slept under the open skies with the *campesinos*. None of them seemed aware it was the Minister of Agriculture they shared their food and drink with. Not that it mattered; the only authority that held any power or influence over the affairs of men anymore was Xiuhtecuhtli, the angry God of Fire.

The situation in the capital city was just as chaotic. Between the clouds of volcanic ash plastering the outer suburbs and the almost continual tremors, existence had relegated to daily survival, and supplies were running out. Rivers of red hot lava were pouring down the slopes of Xiuhtecuhtli, and the capital city lay right in their path.

I made it to the airport and flashed my passport to a gentleman who was obviously an official of the US embassy. "I gotta get on that plane!"

"Who are you?"

"I'm a US citizen!"

"Yeah, but are you connected to the embassy?" he shouted over the noise and confusion. "This is an official flight. Embassy officials only."

To hell with that. "I'm the Minister of Agriculture!" I shouted.

He must have thought I said I'm involved with working with the Ministry of Agriculture, some kind of humanitarian operation. Whatever he thought didn't matter, the man waved me by and I was able to get a seat on what turned out to be the last flight out of there. My last sight of San Cristobal through the passenger window was what looked like a barrage of red hot boulders landing on the far side of the runway and exploding, sending shards of volcanic debris in all directions. I felt sorry for the poor souls left behind. Who wouldn't? It was like the Last Days of Pompeii.

Back in The World my employers didn't have much to say to me. The back-pay they owed me made the ass-chewing bearable, and I still had my arm. Still do, in fact. The hallucinations seemed to have quieted down a bit, or at least they're manageable, which makes me wonder how much of the whole thing really happened and how much was some kind of waking dream – going right back to the beginning, the encounter on the plane, the one-armed man?

"You still worried about losing an arm?" Mike asked, pouring his guest another beer.

"Nah," he said, looking at his arm as he flapped it like a wing. "The only thing I'm worried about is the when and where, and the pain. I lose this arm and I win the lottery."

"How so?"

"I got it insured." He coughed, a bit of a hack, and a gob of some kind spittle flew out, landed at the foot of the bar. Mike glanced down and saw . . . a tiny little yellow snail, with a purple line that followed the spiral of its shell . . .

Chapter 12

The Cement Business

"Hey, Buddy."

Mike looked across the bar and smiled. It was Erik, an old friend from his former life.

"Erik! I haven't seen you in donkey's ears!"

"Years," Erik smiled. "Yeah, Mike, it's been a long time."

"Where was it? Bragg?"

"Last time we saw each other was Stuttgart, I think. Tail end of that mess down in Bosnia."

"Yeah! Shit, that must have been damn near twenty years ago! Welcome to the Long Bar!"

"Thanks, Mike. Do you have any vacancies?"

"You're in luck, its off-season."

"Good. I'd like to rent one of your bungalows, long term."

"Sure, no problem. What have you been up to?"

"Well, let me tell you – because if you're going to put me up, then it's only fair you know the story I'm about to tell," Erik said cryptically.

Mike poured his latest patron a beer, placed it in front of him. "Go on . . ."

"You've heard of North N'enka?"

"Oh yeah," Mike said. "the World's Newest Nation. They just got started, less than five years ago, right?"

"Yeah, and they're about to become Africa's next failed state."

"That bad, huh?"

"Worse . . ." Erik took a pull on his beer, set it down. "Se' was never anything more than a sleepy colonial outpost, a nowheresville, end of the line for civilization. It was where British influence ended, the furthest boundary of the French Empire, and the northernmost edge of the national-level train wreck that was Belgian experiment in Africa. Then suddenly Se' became the capital city of the brand-new nation of North N'enka. Now its a mushrooming, sprawling mess of new construction combined with the worst roads of any city in Africa, if not the world. They have a total of about 500 meters of paved road, which run between the Presidential Palace and the American Embassy. This is in a city of several million, in a nation the size of Illinois.

"Due to the dropping price of oil, revenues that were counted on when they established their new country failed to appear. There is an incredibly inverted supply and demand situation that's driven inflation up to about 700%.

"Because of the demand for construction materials, for example, a fifty-pound bag of cement - which normally goes for between five to twenty US dollars, depending on how many bags you're buying – can go for as much as two hundred bucks, or even more. And every bag of cement in the country has to be flown in over the border – which is pricey, but cheaper than trucking it in, actually."

"How can that possibly be? Moving cement by air is cheaper than by truck?"

"People fail to realize how incredibly big Africa is. Distances are vast, and you simply cannot get anything accomplished without airfreight. Not on any significant level, that is.

"The only roads that exist out there are potholed red dirt tracks. And of course, the security situation is absolutely in the toilet." Erik took another pull on his beer.

"Naturally," Mike replied.

"When the country first stood up it was organized with the assistance of the US and the EU and of course the UN, and everything was looking like a success path. Then the army split up along tribal lines."

"Fancy that," Mike quipped. "Never would have seen that coming."

"Regiments and battalions went to whoever was their tribal loyalty loyal; the president, or whichever vice-president represents their tribe. There are six vice-presidents, by the way.

"Then there's the police - which are actually another military organization, only they wear blue uniforms instead of camouflage - and the National Security Service, the NSS - which is in reality yet another military organization, masquerading as an intelligence service.

"What all these various military and para-military organizations do is basically to set up roadblocks and collect "taxes". They're not capable of conducting any kind of maneuver warfare - mostly because they don't have enough gasoline or bullets. And of course they don't have any kind of training, no idea how to do anything but behave like a criminal organization in uniform.

"Sounds like a mess," Mike commented.

"It is," Erik replied. "Even the usual 'independent contractor' security-types are very reluctant to show up, because the situation is so fragmented. It's a no-win situation.

"The UN is present, of course. Their mission is to take care of the refugees. The first thing they did was build a big, sprawling perimeter to hide behind, to protect themselves, right next to the airport. Then they built a big refugee camp right next to their perimeter. The refugee camp has become ever-expanding, like their perimeter, which has become their raison-d'etre for being there in the first place."

"So what were you doing over there, Erik?"

"I was working for an NGO, actually. A humanitarian organization."

This produced a raised eyebrow from Mike.

"Yeah, I could hardly believe it myself, but it was what it was," Erik responded. "While I was there I saw the market for cement and construction materials, and figured I could help these people out a whole hell of a lot better by throwing a little free enterprise their way, rather than handing out sacks of rice and beans."

"And make a little money while you're at it, right?" Mike said. "That's the way of the world."

"Yes, it occurred to me that the business to get into over there was to start up a cement factory. I saw an opportunity, and so I reached out to some of my contacts, guys who had the knowledge and wherewithal, and talked to some people who had the seed money."

"How'd it go?"

"Pretty good at first. I made a business plan, put together a team, scrounged up some seed cash from Erik Baron (the notorious founder of BearPaw) . . ."

"You KNOW Erik Baron?"

"Yes, I know Erik Baron. I've been doing the independent contracting thing for a long time, since the beginning of it all. I was a plank holder, on the original team at BearPaw. Anyway, I got the locals organized, arranged for one of the tribal armies to provide security, and we went about business."

"Sounds cool."

"Well, I learned a lot about cement. Turns out producing cement is not a complex operation – the Romans were doing it, after all. The technology is really low end – a bunch of rock crushing equipment and mixers. It was actually cheaper for us to buy a used cement factory in the States, take it apart and ship it over piece by piece, rather than pay for brand-new off-the-shelf equipment.

"Of course, this involved driving it in overland from the nearest port, which was two countries over. We simply could not fly this stuff in by air. This is where things started getting complicated."

"Sooner or later they always do."

"I oversaw the overland movement myself, and reached out to some contacts for some security personnel. The locals are simply not reliable."

"You get some talent?"

"Yes, I had four ex-Green Berets, and four ex-Foreign Legionnaires."

"Wow, that's some talent!"

"Yeah. Had my hands full riding herd on them, too, let me tell you."

"I can imagine!"

"Didn't have any trouble with the Legionnaires. They do what they're told. The fucking Green Berets, nothing but trouble."

"Really? I would have thought it the other way around."

"The Legionnaires do what they're told. All you got to know is when to turn them on and turn them off. The Legion has its own rules of engagement, which are NO rules of engagement, of course. The operative phrase with my Legionnaires was '*Ne tirez pas encore*' - hold fire."

"Oh my God."

"Yeah, they tend to shoot first and ask questions later."

"Holy shit!"

"Yeah, well, it's the Legion, after all."

"What's the problem with the Green Berets? They're supposed to be the best of the best."

"Yeah, well they are. The problem is they want to discuss and analyze every damn thing. They're good for being in charge, I guess, but lousy at being told what to do.

"Anyway, we got the stuff moved overland, then we had to put it together. Imagine a bunch of Legionnaires and Green Berets pouring over plans and trying to assemble a cement factory like kids with an Erector Set, or some of those crazy things you buy at Ikea."

"Ha!"

"We finally got it done, and things were going fine. We were crushing rock and making cement like gangbusters. The trouble with starting any kind of profitable enterprise in a place like that, of course, is sooner or later the police or one of the armies will show up, ransack and loot the place."

"Sounds like things are getting pretty bad over there."

"Well it gets worse," Erik began, pausing to take a deep pull on his beer. "You heard about that bit of nasty business they had there last August?"

"A bit of a shoot-up in the capital city, wasn't it?"

"Yeah. One of the vice-presidents - there are six vice-presidents, each one represents one of the tribes or groups of tribes, and they're all at war against each other - well, one of the vice-presidents, the most powerful vice-president, was in town for peace talks with the President. What happened was, while they were sitting down in the Presidential Palace, their bodyguards got into a firefight with each other."

"Holy shit!"

"Yeah. It didn't go very well for the vice-president's crew. They basically got slaughtered. Being in the heart of the capital city, the president's guys had all kinds of reinforcements. And after they wiped out the vice-president's guys, it was time to loot the local ex-pat liquor store."

"Right," said Mike, refreshing Erik's drink.

"And after they got their drink on, it was time to go ransack the big hotel where all the important ex-pats stay."

"How bad was that?"

"Pretty bad. The women were given a choice. Either have sex with the soldiers, or get raped anyway and then get a bullet in the head. They pack-raped about twenty women – Americans and Europeans - multiple times. And by multiple times, I mean fifteen or twenty times each."

"Holy . . ."

"Yep."

"What about the UN? Don't they have peacekeepers over there?"

"The UN sat on their asses and did nothing. It took them almost six hours to get their Quick Reaction Force – QRF – to roll out there, and by the time they showed up, the North N'enka Peoples Liberation Army rolled a tank out in the street and started launching rounds in their direction. That was the end of the UN's involvement. They skedaddled back to their perimeter out by the airport and sat on their asses with their thumbs up their bum holes."

"Damn."

"Yep. Meanwhile, things were going according to schedule at the cement plant. I mean, an old cement plant doesn't look sexy, we weren't drawing any attention from the local powers-that-be. We were buying raw materials from people in the interior who now suddenly had a source of income, scraping up the rocks and volcanic ash around them, and turning it all into cement, and selling it at a tenth of the price of the stuff they were moving in by air. Everyone's a winner, right?"

"Can't argue with success."

"Yeah, well that was where and when the problems began. We became so successful that local powers-that-be started getting jealous - they wanted a piece of the action, right? My people were afraid to come to work for the cement outfit, due to "payroll taxes" imposed at the roadblocks. But wait it gets worse.

"There are six vice-presidents, right? Well, five of them were pissed off at me, and they're pressuring the President. But I saw this coming, of course, and so I made sure I paid "special taxes" to the President, right from the git-go. What I didn't anticipate was to counter all this grumbling he was getting from his counterparts, the President of the Republic of North N'enka went and made me a Field Marshall in his Army."

"Woah!"

"Yeah, talk about winning the booby prize. All I wanted to do was make an honest buck, and maybe help people out while I was at it. Now I'm a part of the problem, not a part of the solution. Pretty soon it was like having a tiger by the tail.

"Field Marshall is a rank of distinction, of course. Sort of like making Sergeant Major in our Army. There was a bit of a ceremony that went with it."

"I can only imagine what drill and ceremony looks like in a place like that."

"Let me tell you, the ceremony lasted for ten days."

"Woah!"

"Yeah. They had this big chair, looked like a throne, all carved from a single piece of wood. They had me sit in the chair, and for ten days they beat the drums and these Vestal Virgins in white dresses danced in front of me, going into a trance-like state."

"O-k-a-a-a-y . . ."

"There was a bit of palm wine involved. I try to avoid that stuff. It ain't exactly Single Malt."

Mike made a face. Anyone who's ever sampled palm wine would understand.

"In front of me they put this stick, in a stand. It was a big affair, with carvings and beads, and a mummified dog's paw hanging down, and this little skull that for all the world looked like a human skull. If a human was about eighteen inches tall, that is."

"Hmmm. What was the stick for?"

"They told me it was for my grii-grii – my magic, right? Sort of like a medicine pouch. For ten days they beat the drums and the Vestal Virgins danced and gyrated. It's like they were charging it up, like a car battery, right?"

"Oh, okay," Mike said. "Makes sense. What happened after ten days?"

"Oh, on the tenth day the big witch doctor presents the stick to me and tells me that now I've got very strong magical powers, and the stick is my grii-grii. I already figured the stick part out, of course, but the magical powers were a new angle."

"Uh, what are your magical powers?" Mike asked.

"Well, when he presented the stick, the witch doctor told me that I wasn't fully there yet."

"What? More ceremony?"

"No. He said that I first needed to find out what kind of animal I am. He said my animal would come to me, sometime over the course of the next six months or so, and when it came to me, then I would know what kind of animal I am."

"So, what kind of animal are you?"

"Hang on, I'll get to that part."

"Now, in Africa when you rise to the level of any sort of success or prominence – anything from dogcatcher to customs inspector or, in my case, Field Marshall – you're expected to share the wealth. First it's your family, then it's your village, then it's your tribe; they all come with their hand out. And you're expected to share the wealth.

"Well I wasn't from there, I don't have a tribe, but my local troops didn't see it that way; as far as they were concerned, I was a defacto honorable member of their tribe, the Nkasha tribe – I mean, I was a Field Marshall in the Nkasha Army, right? - and as such was expected to shell out the baksheesh.

"Meanwhile, the police and their own tribal soldiers were up to their usual mischief, setting up their illegal roadblocks and collecting "taxes". What they were doing was, when they'd made enough to cover the groceries, they'd take off their uniforms and rent them out - along with their rifles - and go lay under the tree and drink palm wine for the rest of the day.

"Well it turned out that only half my tribal army was present at any given time, and in the afternoons they were all gone. They were out there doing the roadblock stunt as well, pulling the afternoon shift while the other guys lay under the tree.

"So when all hell broke loose, it was just me and my inner core of mercenaries – we were all we had to defend ourselves. The cement plant was too large, though. We'd seen this coming, so we fell back inside an inner perimeter we'd made out of fifty-five gallon drums, filled with cement, of course.

"Holy shit, that's some heavy shit!" Mike exclaimed.

"Ah, it wasn't that bad. You know how it is with those soldiers over there. The safest place to be when they're shooting at you is right where they're aiming. If you try to run or hide, you'll catch a bullet, but if you're right out there in the middle of the street, they'll never hit you. They can't hit the broad side of a barn, from the inside."

"True."

"But it was Zulu Dawn – we were surrounded. Sooner or later we were going to have to break out and fight our way out. We had to get out of Dodge.

"We couldn't make our way to the airport because that's the UN had their perimeter, and the UN had already determined we were an illegal standing army, a band of international adventurers masquerading as a part of the local Ministry of Defense."

"Man, that's complicated."

"Yeah, like they say; 'When you're up to your ass in alligators, it's difficult to remember that your initial objective was to drain the swamp.' Right?"

"So what did you do?"

"We did a deception attack, sent a bunch of fireworks and 40mm in one direction, and while they were all ducking for cover and cowering, we broke out in the opposite direction. We had to fight our way overland, south to the border. It wasn't so much a struggle against armed opposition as it was a sort of symbolic tribal warfare. Whenever we crossed into the next tribal lands

– and North Nkasha has sixty-four different tribes - the local forces would put up a bit of a resistance for show, but then they'd scatter when they saw us advancing on them, fire-and-maneuver.

"How long did it take?"

"The better part of six months."

"Woah."

"Yeah, people really do not realize how incredibly big Africa is. Distances are vast, and getting our hands on diesel fuel was not easy. There simply is not a lot of supply out there, and the locals were asking top dollar. They knew we needed it, and they had it. Law of Supply and Demand at its finest."

"What did you eat?"

"Dog, mostly. At one point we managed to barter for some local cattle and for a while we had beef. At one point we were living off baboon meat. That added environmental crimes to my rap sheet. Baboons are an endangered species, apparently. Who'd have known? There's no shortage of the bastards, and in packs they're as dangerous to humans as hippo or cape buffalo."

"Whats baboon taste like?"

"Not bad actually. Sort of tastes like, you know, chicken."

Mike winced.

"When we got to the border, a new set of problems. The southern border is this huge river, and the whole place was in flood. The bad guys were packing up on us, getting closer. They knew we had a ton of money with us, the pile we made at the cement plant, and they were getting bolder, now that they saw we were trapped. We had to find a way across."

"What did you do?"

"Well, it happened when I was making a recon, up and down the river. We had to find a crossing, a place to ford the river. Because of the flood, the river was more than a mile across in places.

"So I went into the forest, see if there was a place where it narrowed out. It was just myself and two of the guys. We drove as far as the track went, then I got out, told the guys to hang back with the vehicle, and I struck out on foot.

"I was keeping the river to my left but was out of site of the vehicle, way off track, middle of nowhere in the jungle when I had this . . . encounter."

"What kind of encounter?"

"I didn't see it or even hear it at first. It was like I felt it. The whole forest became silent – the birds, the monkeys, the insects even, and I sensed its presence."

"What?"

"Leopard, coming out of a huge tree, right in front of me."

"Oh shit."

"Yeah, and stupid me, I'd left my firearms in the front of the bloody truck."

"Oh double shit."

"Yeah. Leopard is badass. I've seen a leopard haul a zebra carcass up a tree, so it wouldn't have to share with the lions and the hyenas. Leopards are just as bad as lions. Sudden death.

"I watched the cat move down the tree like a stream of molten gold poured from a goldsmith's ladle. Spotted molten gold. All I had was my knife in my hand, and I was holding it with a death-grip. There was fear, but I couldn't allow myself to give in to it. I knew there would be only one chance, a single split second, to survive what was guaranteed to be the fight of my life. It was gonna be me or the cat, there was no way out . . .

"Then the damnedest thing happened."

"What happened?"

"The cat stopped and stared at me, and for some reason I couldn't explain to you now, I knew then and there that I was in no danger.

"The leopard came forward and actually rubbed its head against my leg, for all the world like a giant pussy cat. It let me rub its head and it actually PURRED."

"No way!"

"I'm lyin', I'm dyin'. I don't know how long it lasted, this encounter with the leopard. It was like time stood still. And then – you're going to think this next part is crazy."

"What happened next?"

"The leopard looked up at me, and it was like it was talking to me."

"Wh-a-a-a . . . ?"

"It wasn't moving its mouth or actually saying anything, it was like a voice in my head, only it was the leopard."

"What did it say?"

"It told me there was a crossing, a mile or so back in the other direction, that my army and me could make it across, vehicles and all. It told me to look for the big baobab tree, that was the place."

"Did it, was there a crossing?"

"Yes, exactly like the big cat said." Erik said, taking a pull of his beer. "I had obviously found my animal, the one the witch doctor had told me about."

"Obviously. So how'd it go from there?"

"We never would have found it by ourselves, the crossing. I caught glimpses of the leopard as it escorted us back upriver to where we rejoined the main body. The strange creature was always there, watching us, but always hanging back in the tree line. In fact it was as if I could only see it in my peripheral vision.

"And then we came to the large baobab tree the big cat had described. This was the crossing point.

"Myself and another man walked in front of the vehicles as we slowly made our way across the river. The river was very wide at that point, almost two miles across, but at no point was the water any deeper than eighteen inches. Our vehicles were quite capable of managing this, and the bottom was firm. It was a perfect ford. We never would have found our way across, in a million years.

"We'd made it safely across the border. Home free, almost. When we got to the other side we made a show of us ditching our weapons, as we sought sanctuary across the other side. We held on to our sidearms, of course, tucked beneath our tunics. You never trust anyone in that part of the world. At least, trust, but always have insurance.

We proceeded to the small colonial-style building that was the Customs House. Number Two and myself collected up everyone's passports and went inside.

"There were two officials in there, wearing 1940s-era uniforms and berets. The ranking one was seated behind a rickety wooden desk, his assistant stood off to the side. The flag of their country was draped on the wall over a portrait of the President of their country and the ubiquitous motto stenciled beneath: "Liberté - Égalité - Fraternité". An ancient ceiling fan rotated slowly overhead.

"The two customs officers examined our passports and ourselves with equal curiosity. We weren't their usual customers. They queried where we had come from and how long we wished to stay, and why we did not have visas already stamped in our passports.

"We must have been quite a sight in our bedraggled clothes and the effects of all those weeks in the bush. I'm sure they weren't quite sure if we were white men, or wild men.

"The ranking official finally announced his decision: "*Non.*" We were not refugees, as we claimed, in fact we were mercenaries and there would be no sanctuary for us.

"We pleaded, of course - to go back would be certain death - but the official was firm. He put his hand up, "*Non,*" and then he folded his arms across his chest. He looked down, not even giving us the benefit of eye contact.

"Right. Time to up the ante a bit, perhaps? I reached into my pack and pulled out a thick wad of cash. Perhaps there is a fee for the visas? Not a bribe, a gift? If I place this amount in the desk and leave it there, who is to say who took it - if it was even there in the first place?

"The answer was still the same: "*Non. Ce n'est tout simplement pas possible.*" As he slid the pile of money and our passports across the desk towards us, we were told to go back to where we came from.

"I couldn't believe it. I'd placed what must have been a years' pay for that guy on the desk in front of him, and I'd never seen a minor African functionary in the middle of nowhere turn down a '*cadeau*'. And yet it was what it was. We were being denied entry, and yet going back was not an option.

"I'm not exactly sure what happened next, but there was a loud scream and a blur of yellow and black and suddenly the desk was upended, the chair went flying and the two customs officials were out the door, with the leopard hot on their tracks. It all happened so fast I never even got a proper look at the leopard.

"When I recovered my wits I was outside in the hot sunlight, on my hands and knees, looking down at the dust and breathing hard. One of the customs officers lay before me, bleeding out from deep lacerations about the neck and shoulders. The other official lay a few feet away, he was missing his head altogether. Their bodies were ripped to shreds - the leopard had really done a number on them.

"I got up, shook my head to clear it - I felt as if I had just woke up, as if I had passed out when the leopard had appeared and was just now coming to. I went back inside the Customs House.

"The room was destroyed, of course, and Number Two was looking at me like I was a ghost, all wide-eyed. This caused me to glance down at myself. Somehow or other I had blood all over my hands and forearms. I went into the little washroom off to the side and the image that greeted me in the mirror . . . There was blood everywhere.

"I mean, I was covered in blood. There was blood EVERYWHERE, from my hairline all the way down. Lots of blood. And yet, not a scratch on me.

"I cleaned up as best I could and went back to where Number Two had righted the desk and was sorting out the passports.

"All the necessary stamps were there, so we gave ourselves six-month multiple entry visas, for all our men, and then we got the hell out of there."

"There weren't any problems after the leopard . . . did its thing . . . on the customs officers?"

"We somehow got away with it, incredibly. As soon as we'd made some distance, we pulled the vehicles off road, made a little perimeter, and I paid my guys. I split up the loot even-steven. I mean, the fact was we'd been through a lot more than they'd ever signed on for, so I only saw it as fair. They'd stood by me, so I stood by them."

"That was generous of you."

"Maybe. Another way to look at it was, if it wasn't for everybody pulling as a team, we never would have gotten out of there alive. And because everybody had kept their wits about them and soldiered hard, we hadn't lost anyone. The contract had changed, and I was paying it back."

"Good karma."

"Exactly." Erik took another pull of his beer. "I told the guys if they wanted to get out of there, go back to The World, they were free to go. If they wanted to stick around, I told them I was looking for the next thing. Incredibly, nobody was in a hurry to leave the Continent.

"It was obvious we couldn't hang together like some kind of armed force. Everybody agreed it probably wasn't a good idea, with those funny visas in our passports, to try to leave the country through the international airport, and nobody was eager to do a cross-country move again, not any time soon. So we made a plan to keep in touch, then we split up."

"You're good now?"

"Well that's half the story – because now I had this formidable mercenary army, which Erik Baron suddenly showed interest in. He had uses for my guys in other situations in the middle of Africa. The mess in Libya, etcetera."

"What are you doing for Baron, if you don't mind me asking?"

"Anything and everything. Normally I'd draw the line at any kind of illegal activities, but where there's no law and order, what's illegal? Wherever there's oil and other industry that needs security, or special needs of a client."

"Special needs?"

"Documents and asset recovery. Or if a local politician needs persuading. I draw the line at anything that looks like murder or assassination – we are not hitmen - although we have engaged in armed conflict.

"We fall outside of The Hague and Geneva Conventions, of course, so anything we're involved in a conflict zone is by definition a criminal act.

"Whenever things get hairy, or some kind of legal challenge presents itself, the leopard shows up and we somehow find a way out of it."

"The leopard's still with you?"

"Never went away. The leopard is my animal, just like they told me," Erik said, quietly. "You know, it's strange, Mike. I know it sounds completely weird, but it's just like whenever a situation starts to develop and things start to go south, BAM. The leopard shows up out of nowhere and turns the place into a swirling turbulence of beautiful chaos. At some point I come to, the leopard is gone, and whatever death and destruction it wrought is all over me."

Erik looked up at Mike, haunted. "It's like . . ." He dared not say any more.

Erik stared out across the room, into the darkness beyond the large doors that opened to the huge deck.

"You know," he said, almost wistfully, "The irony of the whole thing is that I started out as a contractor for a humanitarian organization, and all I tried to do was help the people of North N'enka and at the same time make a buck in the cement & hardware business. Yet somehow I ended up becoming a notorious mercenary warlord, and Public Enemy Number One. All I ever tried to do was defend myself and my men, when all these criminals in uniform turned their attentions on to us."

"Things are good now? I mean, you're here, after all."

"Well, actually, there's a problem. I need a place to cool my heels, and that's why I told you this story.

"I'm the former ranking officer of the People's Army of the Republic of North N'enka, and a fugitive war criminal, on the UN lists, wanted by Interpol, and of course Greenpeace and the World Wildlife Fund."

"Holy shit!"

"Yeah," Erik shrugged. "What can I say? It's kind of nice to be popular, eh?"

"Well, you never did do things by half-measures, Erik."

"Yeah. Well, if you take me in I'll cause you no trouble. I'll pay in cash, six months down as a security deposit and six months in advance. There are no banking ties, nothing electronic, and I promise you I will not conduct any business out of your premises. Whaddya say?"

Mike thought about it for a minute. "Can you assure me none of your money is from drugs – narcotics – or human trafficking?"

"Oh yeah, Mike. I don't mess with that shit. Never have, never will. What I've got I earned fair and square. In the cement business, actually. And now these contracts which Baron is setting me up with."

"Then I have no problem with it," Mike said. "All I ask is that, like you said, no business is conducted here on the premises. And if anybody comes sniffing around for you, I don't know who the hell it is they're looking for and I sure as hell ain't gonna tell 'em where to find you."

"Thanks Mike."

"Nothing to it. Blood is thicker than water. You're in 2B. I'll tell Leena Wan in the morning, she keeps track of the books."

"Thanks. How can I help you out? What can I do for you?"

"I'll think of something."

Erik reached across the bar and shook Mike's hand. "Thanks, Mike. You won't be sorry, I can assure you." He shouldered his bag and made his way out the bar, across the wide deck and down the stairway towards bungalow 2B.

Much later, cleaning up the bar, Mike looked out the wide doors to the darkness beyond the deck, the inky darkness. The surf pounding at the rocky shoreline, way down at the bottom of the cliff, made it's eternal booming, like a giant orchestra of native drums far in the distance. And somewhere out there, Mike swore he heard something he hadn't heard in years, and certainly had never heard on this particular stretch of jungled coastline.

Somewhere out in the cold distance, the scream of a large wild cat.

Chapter 13

Casino

Morning in the Cliff Hotel, overlooking the Andaman Sea. Mike sat at his laptop, struggling with his writer's block. He usually worked in a more private part of the hotel, but given that it was rainy season and the hotel was almost empty, Mike was seated at a far table on the wide veranda. And normally, nobody bothered him; he was obviously busy at work. This morning the Blonde Woman approached him.

"May I?" she asked, indicating a seat at the table.

Resigning himself to another fruitless morning of writer's block, Mike sighed. "You may as well."

"What are you doing?"

"I'm writing."

"No you're not. You're just sitting there looking at your computer. If you were writing, I wouldn't have come over."

"Okay."

"So what are you not writing about?"

"I dunno. Keep getting stuck between what I want to write and a dozen concepts going around in my head."

"So what is it you want to write?"

"I always wanted to write adventure novels, spin yarns like the great heroic writers; Alistair MacLean, Frederick Forsythe, Ian Fleming. MacLean's Where Eagles Dare is total, one hundred percent gutsy he-man adventure."

"Good writers. Successful, you can't argue with that. Are they your literary influences, though?"

"Not really. I suppose my influences are Conrad, for his dark introspective side. Hemingway, of course, for style of writing, and Somerset Maugham captures irony so well."

"Those writers all lived and died a long time ago. Will your tale occur in their time era, or will it be contemporary?"

"I don't know. I imagine my favorite time era of history is the late 30s-40s-early 50s."

"Ah, the Noir genre," the Blonde Woman stated. Mike sensed approval. "What can you write of those times?"

Mike thought for a bit. "Well, there's a place I've been, it's like time stood still, somewhere back in the thirties or forties. Had quite an adventure there, actually."

"There you go," said the Blonde Woman. "Tell me about it."

"Well, I needed a vacation. Around here," Mike indicated the veranda, the jungled cliff, "existence is vacation-like, but everyone needs a change of scenery every now and then."

"A vacation from a vacation. Not an unheard-of concept."

"Looking for something really different, I took the train to Bangkok and rode it all the way up to Chiang Mai. It's an overnight trip."

"Riding the trains in Thailand is an adventure in and of itself," the Blonde Woman offered.

"Quite. As the train stops at every little station along the way, a small army of hawkers come on board the train. They walk up and down the aisle selling bamboo tubes full sticky rice sealed with folded banana leaf plugs, whole barbecued chickens, de-boned and splayed out in bamboo frames, and that sweet ice tea in plastic bags tied up with rubber bands and a straw poking out the top. For less money than the price of the taxi it takes to get to the station, a guy can feast like a king all the way up to Chiang Mai.

"After we pulled into Chiang Mai, the old northern capital, I made my way through the bustling marketplace to the bus station, caught the bus up to Chiang Rai, the real heart of Northern Thailand.

"I wandered around town, enjoyed the bright sunshine, found a little open-air restaurant with folding chairs and tables and had some lunch. After the meal, I walked down to the marketplace and took a smaller, more dilapidated bus to a really remote town right at the very top of Thailand; the Golden Triangle.

"Mae Sai was just what I was looking for; the whole town looks like time stopped in the forties. I stayed in a little bungalow just off the main drag. At the end of the street was the wooden bridge, across the river was Burma. The view out the back window of my place was rice paddies, coconut palms and beyond that the mountains; the foot hills of the Himalayas.

"While I was there I got some kind of dry-eye irritation. My eyes really started to bother me. In search of some eye drops, the only place that remotely resembled some kind of pharmacy was this ancient Chinese apothecary. . .

"The old lady in the apothecary looked like she was a thousand years old. She was blabbering away, no kind of language I had any knowledge of. Didn't sound like any kind of Chinese even, what little I know of the Chinese languages.

"She pressed into my hand a small brown glass bottle with mysterious label all printed out in Chinese characters . . . I asked her how much, she waved her hand, babbled something that obviously meant it was nothing, gratis, free. On the house. I pressed a handful of baht into her hands, thanked her, bowed and left the apothecary.

"The eye drops that the old Chinese lady sold me had a strange effect. I first noticed it the next morning, in the hallway to the washroom. I looked a Thai man in the eyes. Suddenly there was a strange sensation; it was like I was flashing on myself."

"What do you mean?"

"Like I could see myself. Like I was looking in the mirror. Only there was no mirror.

"I started seeing strange things, other . . . perspectives. I glanced at a dog in the street and now I had the vision of the dog, from the dog's eye-view. I glanced at a hawk overhead and suddenly a bubble vision of the entire street, seen from above. My eyes were like binoculars and I could read a newspaper from across the street. It was like some kind of strange side effect of the eye drops. Whatever bird or animal I looked at, now I could see what they see!

"Birds have VERY GOOD eyesight, of course, everybody knows this. It was then that I fully realized that if I looked a person in the eyes, I could see what they were seeing. It was obvious what I must do next . . .

"I went further north, crossed the wooden bridge at Mae Sai, went into the Shan States of Northern Burma, into the area controlled by the Kuomintang – the remnants of Chiang Kai Shek's old Nationalist Army. There is a casino there, of sorts. It was actually a ramshackle wooden building full of Chinese antiques and bric-a-brac.

It was a casino like no other casino I had ever been in; a casino only in that gambling was taking place there. The walls were whitewashed cement, the music was the wailing of Chinese opera over tinny speakers. Empty drink bottles stood clustered beneath the tables. Cardboard boxes and packing crates stacked high indicated the large room's actual intended purpose; it was a warehouse, a go-down.

The corners of the room were dark. Bare electric bulbs provided pools of bright light around the tables where the gamblers played with manic intensity. They played an Asian game with decks of cards that seemed to have an indeterminate number of suits, exclaiming out loud as they throw down a winning card, "*Haw!*"

"*Chai Yoh!*"

I was the only westerner in the place.

Shadowy figures moved about the corners. I was a guest of the Triads, the infamous Chinese mafia. The go-down was the Triad's headquarters. There were items stacked high to the ceiling; flat screen televisions, fans, rice cookers, laptop computers. This was their loot, the bounty of the black market.

"One should never enter the casino unless one is feeling good, confident and happy in life. I was feeling good because I was on vacation, and self-confidence is what brought me to the casino. Happiness is a relative concept. 'Oh well, I guess I got two out of three going for me,' I thought as I took a seat at the large table in the middle of the room. I threw down some money and indicated for the dealer to deal me in. The Triads glanced at each other, silently assessing my joining their game. The dealer nodded, and I was in.

"The game was a version of gin rummy, or maybe closer to a cards version of mah jong. I was able to figure it out quickly enough, and of course with the eyesight thing I was able to see the other players' cards. Needless to say I started making money at the table. A LOT of money.

"This eventually drew a lot of negative attention of the Triads, of course. There was intrigue . . . stress and anxiety. They couldn't prove anything on me but they were pissed off. REALLY pissed off. So finally they dragged me into the back room, their offices.

An older Chinese guy wearing a loose-fitting singlet with suspenders was interviewing me; thin to the point of emaciation, balding, peering at me over his reading glasses with a cigarette dangling from his lips. Or rather, he was interrogating me. During the course of my interrogation the younger ones pacing around, waving around their Colt .45 automatic pistols - which look like artillery pieces in their little hands.

In another section of the warehouse, the Triads were getting their tattoos worked on. They all had these huge back tattoos; dragons and phoenixes and Chinese goddesses floating in clouds with silk scarves trailing behind them. One of them had a Venus de Milo that covered his entire back. The entire scene was really out of this world. Or at least I thought so at the time, until what happened next.

"What happened next?" the Blonde Woman asked.

"Eventually, I guess the Triads couldn't decide whether to kill me, or just kick me out of there . . . that's when the Dragon Lady made her entrance.

"The Dragon Lady?"

"She's their charismatic leader," Mike said. "She wields some kind of mysterious control over the Triads. They scurried out of the way when she entered the room, avoiding eye contact. She had them release me with a nod of her head, had me taken to the bathroom to get cleaned up.

"Just before they were going to escort me to the door, Dragon Lady noticed me putting in my eye drops. She said, 'Wait a minute boys – I've seen this before . . .'

"Dragon Lady wanted to take control of me, but I could see myself through her eyes, and strangely, I knew how to posture myself to seduce her, seduce the Dragon Lady.

"Meanwhile the Triads boys decided fuck it, if they can't kill me and they can't cut me loose - because Dragon Lady has developed an interest in me - least they're going to do is get me tattooed. Put their mark on me as a warning to others, right? It's an old tradition in the Chinese mafia."

Mike held out his left forearm. "That's how I ended up with this big dragon tattoo."

There was something distinctly odd about the tattoo, almost hypnotic. Anyone who looked at it was drawn into its intricate design. Even the Blonde Woman did a double take at its shiny scales, the way the dragon seemed to almost . . . move . . .

"Meanwhile Dragon Lady was going all googly-goo-goo over me, dragon tattoo and all. The Dragon Lady offered me tea, said if I'd come over to her, between my extraordinary gift of vision and her evil nefarious Triad secret society team, we would rule the criminal underworld of Southeast Asia.

"The tea she served was opium-laced - perhaps something stronger – as were the perfumed cigarettes she offered me, which I accepted. A slight feeling of dizziness, vertigo overcame me. This passed, but then I seemed to transcend to a strange state of consciousness; a hallucinatory, out-of-body state of mind.

"I wasn't sure if the Dragon Lady and I made it together; my memory is patchy on this, almost false memories. I have visions of us lying together, visions of the Dragon Lady in various stages of undress. She is very beautiful, but there is an other-worldly aspect to her. It's as if her body is perfect but something about her lends one to believe – to know beyond doubt! - that she is a thousand years old.

"Her fingernails became elongated and pointy, they appear to be made of silver and gold. Her hair became as long as the silk scarves that trail around the Chinese goddesses as they float in the clouds . . . her eyes were like green orbs of jade . . .

"And as Dragon Lady spoke to me, her lips do not move but her words were ringing in my ears: 'Very few speak of it," she said to me. "The most influential man would speak intelligently well enough in a type of riddle to keep attention so widely, to all audiences . . . including the female glowing with desire . . . you hint of sexuality when building bridges of gold . . . while men of wealth desire that you have a hidden knowledge of how to obtain wealth and fortune . . . you leave us, yet entertained and wanting so much more. Much more, I am willing to invest everything I have to get something that you have. Your style, your allure, what you have is worth more than wealth alone.'

By now we were floating in the air, vertical, face to face yet circling one another. Clouds and long silk scarves and fantastic glowing streaks of colored light circled about us as we circled around and around and around.

"The Dragon Lady continued speaking, her lips not moving, yet her words ringing in my ears. 'You rule the existence of all audiences and no longer do you seek to impress because it is you. You RULE THE WORLD, which is all that you see . . .'

"Now we were above a stormy sea; the sky grew dark as the angry sea boiled beneath us and I saw a dragon cutting through the breaking waves. The dragon moved with great speed and power, coiling and uncoiling as it stirred the sea and intensified the terrible storm lashing all about us.

"Then the creature looked up at Dragon Lady, as loyal as any pet ever was to its mistress. Withdrawing a vial from within her robes, Dragon Lady poured a white liquid down into the dragon's mouth. The dragon's eyelids slowly closed as it was satiated, and it sank beneath the waves. The storm subsided, sunlight began to break through the dark clouds, and the sea grew calm.

"That is when I looked down at the dragon tattoo on my arm and noticed for the first time that it was dancing . . . curling and uncoiling about itself . . . hissing and spitting bits of smoke and fire.

"I finally descended into a deep, black sleep . . .

"When I awoke I was under my mosquito net, in my bungalow back here at the hotel in southern Thailand . .

. bathed in sweat . . . it was as if I just came out of a high fever which had lasted for days.

"How did I get here? Did it all really happen? Or was it only a dream? A hallucination brought on by the effects of whatever medicine it was the old lady sold me at the apothecary? Or perhaps a delirium brought about by a tropical fever?

"Then I looked down at my left forearm and there it was . . . the Dragon Tattoo. It's coiling and uncoiling - just like in my hallucination, or whatever it was - hissing and spitting smoke and fire . . ."

"Excellent," the Blonde Woman said, placing her palms gently down on the table, indicating their conversation was concluded. "You have your story now. All you have to do is write it down."

With that, she got up, straightened out her sarong and smiled.

Then she turned and left the table. The glare of the sun's rays became somehow brighter and whiter despite the green foliage. Mike had to squint and shade his eyes with his hand as the Blonde Woman walked off the veranda to the trail leading to the stairs down to the beach. It must have been the sun playing tricks on his eyes. The Blonde Woman seemed to become a figure of brightness as she retreated, brighter and brighter until there was just bright sunlight, a momentary blinding flash that seared itself on his mind, and when he could see again, the Blonde Woman somehow seemed to dissolve. Then she disappeared forever . . .

A Thousand Drops of Rain – ยดน้ำฟน

Peter Crittenden, 28 August 2015

About the Author

Peter Crittenden is a retired US Army Special Forces NCO, with extensive experience in Southeast Asia, Africa, the Middle East, Eastern Europe, Australia, and the Americas. The son of an Australian ex-pat, Pete grew up in Sumatra, Bangladesh and Thailand. During the course of his military career, among other duties Pete served as a survival instructor at the John F. Kennedy Special Warfare Center and School at Fort Bragg, North Carolina. Since retirement from active duty, Pete has worked as a security consultant and personnel recovery advisor for government agencies and corporate clients.

Nowadays Pete lives in Pennsylvania with his wife Ki, a successful artist. He is the author of *Survival Mindset*.

www.blacksmithpublishingcom

9 781956 904109